Cheshire Libraries
A 81
D0766283

for me the finest examples of high comedy [illegible]
England during the past seventy-five years . . . spectacular'
Sunday Times

'Barbara Pym has a sharp eye for the exact nuances of social behaviour'
The Times

'The wit and style of a twentieth-century Jane Austen'
Harpers & Queen

'Very funny and keenly observant of the ridiculous as well as the pathetic in humanity'
Financial Times

'A spare masterpiece of loneliness in retirement'
Telegraph

'*Quartet in Autumn* is immeasurably her finest work of fiction'
Evening Standard

'An alert miniaturist . . . her novels have a distinctive flavour, as instantly recognisable as Lapsang tea'
Daily Telegraph

Quartet in Autumn

A writer from the age of sixteen, Barbara Pym has been acclaimed as 'the most underrated writer of the century' (Philip Larkin). Pym's substantial reputation evolved through the publication of six novels from 1950 to 1961, then resumed in 1977 with the publication of *Quartet in Autumn* and three other novels. She died in 1980.

Also by Barbara Pym

Some Tame Gazelle
Excellent Women
Jane and Prudence
Less than Angels
A Glass of Blessings
No Fond Return of Love
The Sweet Dove Died
A Few Green Leaves
Crampton Hodnet
An Unsuitable Attachment
An Academic Question
Civil to Strangers

Barbara Pym

Quartet in Autumn

With an introduction by Alexander McCall Smith

CHESHIRE LIBRARIES	
A 81759212 1	
Askews & Holts	12-Nov-2015
AF	£8.99
AFI-G	

PICADOR CLASSIC

First published 1977 by Macmillan London

This Picador Classic edition first published 2015 by Picador
an imprint of Pan Macmillan
20 New Wharf Road, London N1 9RR
Associated companies throughout the world
www.panmacmillan.com

ISBN 978-1-4472-8961-6

Copyright © Barbara Pym 1977
Introduction copyright © Alexander McCall Smith 2015

All rights reserved. No part of this publication may be reproduced, stored in a retrieval system, or transmitted, in any form, or by any means (electronic, mechanical, photocopying, recording or otherwise) without the prior written permission of the publisher.

1 3 5 7 9 8 6 4 2

A CIP catalogue record for this book is available from the British Library.

Printed and bound by CPI Group (UK) Ltd, Croydon, CR0 4YY

This book is sold subject to the condition that it shall not, by way of trade or otherwise, be lent, hired out, or otherwise circulated without the publisher's prior consent in any form of binding or cover other than that in which it is published and without a similar condition including this condition being imposed on the subsequent purchaser.

Visit **www.picador.com/classic** to read more about all our books and to buy them. You will also find features, author interviews and news of any author events, and you can sign up for e-newsletters so that you're always first to hear about our new releases.

Introduction

Quartet in Autumn is the penultimate novel that Barbara Pym published during her lifetime. It appeared in 1977, three years before her death, and some sixteen years after the infamous rejection by her publishers of *An Unsuitable Attachment.* That rejection, which came after she had published six reasonably well-received novels, was a cruel blow and it effectively silenced for fifteen years one of the great comic novelists of the twentieth century, the Jane Austen of our times. Fortunately that silencing was not complete, and she was to be given the time to publish what is considered by many to be the finest of her novels – scant consolation, of course, but at least it meant that when she died in 1980 she had seen the merits of her novels widely recognized and had received the accolade of a Booker Prize nomination.

This delicate and poignant novel was the crowning glory of a literary career that in many respects reflected the author's life. Barbara Pym is surely the finest recorder of lives lived on the margins of a shabby and fading England. Her territory is not the upper-class world of Evelyn Waugh, the country and tennis-set milieu of Betjeman and Benson, or the gritty world of any number of social realist novelists. She describes the life led by middle-aged spinsters, clergymen, and minor officials of what used to be called genteel birth. These are people who are on the fringe of what is happening elsewhere; they are essentially observers who are aware of the richer lives of others but who are conscious of the fact that they will never be a part of that more colourful, more emotionally engaged world. Romance is not for them – yearning is, but not romance.

In many respects Barbara Pym herself did not look like a complete outsider. She was the beneficiary of an Oxford education, she was a published novelist in her thirties, she had a job in an anthropological institute in London, and she enjoyed the friendship of people such as Philip Larkin. It was her self-appointed role, though, to watch rather than to do. This is not unusual in novelists as gifted in wit and perceptive ability as Barbara Pym: if you see the humour in a situation then you are not necessarily one to participate in it. Your role will be to take notes and to bring out the essential poignancy of life that the participants themselves will never see.

Barbara Pym did that throughout her life. She was concerned with the emotional longings of her characters, with their dreams of romance, but she herself never married or had children. At Oxford she had a friend, Henry Harvey, whom she admired, but her passion for him was never requited and settled, in due course, into a comfortable friendship. He married somebody else, and had a second marriage too, both ending in divorce; it was a very Pym-like role for her to be the faithful friend in the background, the person who has to make do with second best.

In her professional life she similarly played a secondary role, working in the International Africa Institute where, as assistant editor of the journal *Africa*, she encountered the models for the anthropologists who feature in the pages of her novels. Her life was perhaps little different from that of many of her characters – a modest life, a life unmarked by major salience, but at the same time a life rich in observation and quiet, dry humour. The self-deprecating thoughts that occur to the likes of Letty and Marcia in *Quartet in Autumn* are the sort of thoughts that one can imagine

Barbara Pym herself harbouring as she lived out her life on the margins of greater things.

Quartet in Autumn is perhaps the most memorable of Barbara Pym's novels because it is the saddest. Its themes are those of growing old and the loneliness and isolation that can come with age. The four protagonists of this book all share an office; they do not have a great deal to do, and indeed on their retirement the office is effectively going to cease to exist. Their fortunes differ: Marcia and Edward are better placed domestically than Norman and Letty, who live in bedsits. Their interests differ: Edwin fills his life with the festivals of Anglo-Catholicism; the others have rather less to occupy their time. They all have their routines, though, and resent interference. This is particularly the case with Marcia, who finds herself irritated by a concerned social worker who is keen to motivate her to mix more. As the tale progresses, their isolation from one another becomes more obvious and more defeating; only at the very end, after one of their number succumbs do we see the survivors getting together – in a very tentative way. The novel, then, ends on a positive note, even if that note is very faint and uncertain. This is not a depressing book, even if the circumstances in which the characters find themselves seem very bleak.

What diminishes the impact of any bleakness is the humour, for which Barbara Pym was justly famous. I find her more amusing than any other twentieth-century writer, including Benson. Benson's Mapp and Lucia novels are highly amusing but Barbara Pym's work has far greater psychological depth, and is therefore much funnier. In this book there is a wonderful episode in which Marcia deals with the issue of a milk bottle passed on to her by Letty. This milk bottle comes from the wrong dairy and is therefore refused by the regular milkman. This incident causes Marcia to dismiss the possibility of ever sharing a roof with Letty, and indeed results in an eventual frosty giving back to Letty of the offending bottle. This is a very small thing, but it assumes major importance – and it is the hallmark of a really great comic writer that a mountain may be made out of such a molehill. But at the same time, it is a very moving moment because it reminds us of the emptiness of a life and the pointlessness of harbouring grudges. We all behave a little bit like that from time to time; we all have something that is the equivalent of that symbolic milk bottle.

In another magnificent scene, Norman goes to the British Museum to look at the mummified crocodiles. That is such a lovely, powerful image, and it says so much about how we look for meaning in the most unlikely places. There is something at once both gloriously comic and profoundly sad about mummified crocodiles and in the fact that anyone should go to see them in the British Museum. It is just the sort of image that Barbara Pym excels in and handles with such a remarkably deft touch. How can one forget such a thing? On my next visit to the British Museum I shall look for them, in homage to Barbara Pym. As she herself would say, 'How reassuring to know that I have been instrumental in persuading at least one person to visit the mummified crocodiles in the British Museum.'

Quartet in Autumn is of particular significance among Barbara Pym's novels in that it includes quite a substantial amount of social comment on the changes in British society that started in the immediate post-war period and gathered pace in the sixties and seventies. The two men and two women in this novel are all, in their different ways, washed up in a place they never thought they would be. London has changed; Englishness has faltered and immigration is on the rise. Letty, in particular, feels this change when the lodging house in which she lives is bought by an overseas family. In one very poignant paragraph, we are made privy to Letty's puzzlement as to how it came about that she, a middle-class Englishwoman born in Malvern in 1914, should find herself in a room in London surrounded by people whose ways are foreign to her and who make a lot of enthusiastic noise. 'It must surely be because she had not married,' we are told. 'No man had taken her away and immured her in some comfortable suburb where . . . nobody was filled with enthusiasm.'

But it is not just that Letty and the others feel that their surroundings are becoming alien to them – the novel also reminds us of the impact of retirement. The retirement party given for the two women is a masterly scene, with a speech being given by a senior colleague that must surely express everything that is distressing about the way those who have given their lives to a company or organization may be so casually consigned to history. Ultimately the only way in which meaning will be injected into these lives is through the recognition by the quartet itself of the need to support one another and find in each other an end to loneliness. That is the message of this exquisitely crafted and utterly haunting novel.

Alexander McCall Smith

One

THAT DAY THE four of them went to the library, though at different times. The library assistant, if he had noticed them at all, would have seen them as people who belonged together in some way. They each in turn noticed him; with his shoulder-length golden hair. Their disparaging comments on its length, its luxuriance, its general unsuitability – given the job and the circumstances – were no doubt reflections on the shortcomings of their own hair. Edwin wore his, which was thin, greying and bald on top, in a sort of bob – 'even older gentlemen are wearing it longer now', his barber had told him – and the style was an easy one which Edwin considered not unbecoming to a man in his early sixties. Norman, on the other hand, had always had 'difficult' hair, coarse, bristly and now iron-grey, which in his younger days had refused to lie down flat at the crown and round the parting. Now he did not have to part it and had adopted a medieval or pudding-basin style, rather like the American crew-cut of the forties and fifties. The two women – Letty and Marcia – had hair as different from each other as it was possible to imagine in the nineteen seventies, when most women in their sixties had a regular appointment at the hairdresser for the arrangement of their short white, grey or dyed red curls. Letty had faded light brown hair, worn rather too long and in quality as soft and wispy as Edwin's was. People sometimes said – though less often now – how lucky she was not to have gone grey, but Letty knew that there were white hairs interspersed with the brown and that most people would have had a brightening 'rinse' anyway. Marcia's short, stiff, lifeless hair was uncompromisingly dyed a harsh dark brown from a bottle in the bathroom cupboard, which she had used ever since she had noticed the first white hairs some thirty years earlier. If there were now softer and more becoming ways of colouring one's hair, Marcia was unaware of them.

Now, at lunchtime, each went about his or her separate business in the library. Edwin made use of *Crockford's Clerical Directory* and also had occasion to consult *Who's Who* and even *Who Was Who*, for he was engaged in serious research into the antecedents and qualifications of a certain clergyman who had recently been appointed to a living in a parish he sometimes frequented. Norman had not come to the library for any literary purpose, for he was not much of a reader, but it was a good place to sit and a bit nearer than the British Museum which was another of his lunchtime stamping grounds. Marcia too regarded the library as a good, free, warm place not too far from the office, where you could sit for a change of scene in winter. It was also possible to collect leaflets and pamphlets setting out various services available for the elderly in the Borough of Camden. Now that she was in her sixties Marcia took every opportunity to find out what was due to her in the way of free bus travel, reduced and cheap meals, hairdressing and chiropody, although she never made use of the information. The library was also a good place to dispose of unwanted objects which could not in her opinion be classified as rubbish suitable for the dustbin. These included bottles of a certain kind, but not milk bottles which she kept in a shed in her garden, certain boxes and paper bags and various other unclassified articles which could be left in a corner of the library when nobody was looking. One of the library assistants (a woman) had her eye on Marcia, but she was unconscious of this as she deposited a small, battered tartan-patterned cardboard box, which had contained 'Killikrankie oatcakes', at the back of a convenient space on one of the fiction shelves.

Of the four only Letty used the library for her own pleasure and possible edification. She had always been an unashamed reader of novels, but if she hoped to find one which reflected her own sort of life she had come to realize that the position of an unmarried, unattached, ageing woman is of no interest whatever to the writer of modern fiction. Gone were the days when she had hopefully filled in her Boots Book Lovers' library list from novels reviewed in the Sunday papers, and there had now been a change in her reading habits. Unable to find what she needed in 'romantic' novels, Letty had turned to biographies of which there was no dearth. And because these were 'true' they were really better than fiction. Not perhaps better than Jane Austen or Tolstoy, which she had not read anyway, but certainly more 'worth while' than the works of any modern novelist.

In the same way, Letty, perhaps because she was the only one of the four who really liked reading, was also the only one who regularly had lunch out of the office. The restaurant she usually patronized was called the Rendezvous but it was not much of a place for romantic meetings. People who worked in the nearby offices crowded in between twelve and two, ate their meal as quickly as possible, and then hurried away. The man at Letty's table had been there when she sat down. With a brief hostile glance he handed her the menu, then his coffee had come, he had drunk it, left 5p for the waitress and gone. His place was taken by a woman who began to study the menu carefully. She looked up, perhaps about to venture a comment on price increases, pale, bluish eyes troubled about VAT. Then, discouraged by Letty's lack of response, she lowered her glance, decided on macaroni au gratin with chips and a glass of water. The moment had passed.

Letty picked up her bill and got up from the table. For all her apparent indifference she was not unaware of the situation. Somebody had reached out towards her. They could have spoken and a link might have been forged between two solitary people. But the other woman, satisfying her first pangs of hunger, was now bent rather low over her macaroni au gratin. It was too late for any kind of gesture. Once again Letty had failed to make contact.

Back in the office Edwin, who had a sweet tooth, bit the head off a black jelly baby. There was nothing racist about his action or his choice, it was simply that he preferred the pungent liquorice flavour of the black babies to the more insipid orange, lemon or raspberry of the others. The devouring of the jelly baby formed the last course of his midday meal which he usually ate at his desk among papers and index cards.

When Letty came into the room he offered her the bag of jelly babies but this was only a ritual gesture and he knew that she would refuse. Eating sweets was self-indulgent, and even though she was now in her sixties there was no reason why she should not keep her spare, trim figure.

The other occupants of the room, Norman and Marcia, were also eating their lunch. Norman had a chicken leg and Marcia an untidy sandwich, bulging with lettuce leaves and slippery slices of tomato. On a mat on the floor the electric kettle was pouring out steam. Somebody had put it on for a hot drink and forgotten to switch it off.

Norman wrapped up his bone and placed it neatly in the wastepaper basket. Edwin lowered an Earl Grey tea bag carefully into a mug and filled it with boiling water from the kettle. Then he added a slice of lemon from a small round plastic container.

Marcia opened a tin of instant coffee and made two mugs of the drink for herself and Norman. There was nothing particularly significant about her action – it was just a convenient arrangement they had. They both liked coffee and it was cheaper to buy a large tin and share it between them. Letty, having had her meal out, did not make herself a drink, but went into the cloakroom and fetched a glass of water which she placed on a coloured hand-worked raffia mat on her table. Her place was by the window and she had covered the window sill with pots of trailing plants, the kind that proliferated themselves by throwing out miniature replicas which could be rooted to make new plants. 'Nature she loved, and next to Nature, Art,' Edwin had once quoted, even going on to finish the lines about her having warmed both hands before the fire of life – but not *too* close, mind you. Now the fire was sinking, as it was for all of them, but was she, or were any of them, ready to depart?

Something of this may have been in Norman's subconscious as he turned the pages of his newspaper.

'Hypothermia,' he read the word slowly. 'Another old person found dead. We want to be careful we don't get hypothermia.'

'It isn't a thing you *get*,' said Marcia bossily. 'Not like catching an infectious disease.'

'Well, if you were found dead of it, like this old woman here, you could say you'd *got* it, couldn't you?' said Norman, defending his usage.

Letty's hand moved over to the radiator and lingered there. 'It's a state or condition, isn't it,' she said, 'when the body gets cold, loses heat or something like that.'

'That's one thing we've got in common then,' said Norman, his snappy little voice matching his small spare body. 'The chance of being found dead of hypothermia.'

Marcia smiled and fingered a leaflet in her handbag, one she had picked up at the library that morning – something about extra heating allowances for the elderly – but she kept the information to herself.

'Cheerful, aren't you,' said Edwin, 'but perhaps there's something in it. Four people on the verge of retirement, each one of us living alone, and without any close relative near – that's us.'

Letty made a murmuring sound, as if unwilling to accept this classification. And yet it was undeniably true – each one lived alone. Strangely enough they had been talking about it earlier that morning when something – again in Norman's paper – had reminded them that Mother's Day was upon them, with the shops full of suitable gifts and the price of flowers suddenly going up. Not that they ever bought flowers, but the increase was noted and commented on. Yet it could hardly affect people too old to have a mother still alive. Indeed, it was sometimes strange to reflect that each of them had once had a mother. Edwin's mother had lived to a respectable age – seventy-five – and had died after a brief illness without giving any trouble to her son. Marcia's mother had died in the suburban house where Marcia now lived alone, in the upstairs front bedroom with the old cat Snowy beside her. She had been eighty-nine, what some might think of as a great age but nothing wonderful or to be remarked on. Letty's mother had died at the end of the war, then her father had married again. Shortly after this her father had died and the stepmother had in due course found another husband, so that Letty now had no connection with the West Country town where she had been born and brought up. She had sentimental and not entirely accurate memories of her mother, wandering round the garden snipping off dead heads, wearing a dress of some floating material. Only Norman had never known his mother – 'Never had a mum,' he used to say in his bitter sardonic way. He and his sister had been brought up by an aunt, and yet it was he who inveighed most fiercely against the commercializing of what had originally been the old country custom of Mothering Sunday.

'Of course you've got your church,' said Norman, addressing Edwin.

'And there's Father Gellibrand,' said Marcia, for they had all heard so much about Father G., as Edwin called him, and they envied Edwin the stable background of the church near Clapham Common where he was Master of Ceremonies (whatever that might be) and on the parochial church council (the PCC). Edwin would be all right, because although he was a widower and lived alone he had a married daughter living in Beckenham, and no doubt she would see to it that her old father wasn't found dead of hypothermia.

'Oh, yes, Father G.'s a real tower of strength,' Edwin agreed, but after all the church was open to everybody. He couldn't understand why neither Letty nor Marcia seemed to go to church. It was easier to see why Norman didn't.

The door opened and a young black girl, provocative, cheeky and bursting with health, entered the room.

'Anything for the post?' she asked.

The four were conscious of the way she looked at them, perhaps seeing Edwin, large and bald with a pinkish face, Norman, small and wiry with his bristly grey hair, Marcia with her general look of oddness, Letty, fluffy and faded, a Home Counties type, still making an effort with her clothes.

'Post?' Edwin was the first to speak, echoing her question. 'Hardly yet, Eulalia. The post does not have to be collected until half past three, and it is now' – he consulted his watch – 'two forty-two precisely. Just trying it on,' he said, when the girl retired, defeated.

'Hoping to get off early, lazy little so-and-so,' said Norman.

Marcia closed her eyes wearily as Norman began to go on about 'the blacks'. Letty tried to change the subject, for it made her uneasy to criticize Eulalia or to be guilty of any unkindness towards coloured people. Yet the girl was irritating and needed to be disciplined, even though there was no doubt that her exuberant vitality was disturbing, especially to an elderly woman who felt herself in contrast to be greyer than ever, crushed and dried up by the weak British sun.

Tea came at last and just before five o'clock the two men packed up what they were doing and went out of the room together, though they would separate on leaving the building, Edwin to the Northern Line for Clapham Common and Norman to the Bakerloo for Kilburn Park.

Letty and Marcia began a more leisurely tidying up. They did not speak of or break into gossip about the two men, who were accepted as part of the office furniture and not considered worthy of comment unless they did something surprisingly out of character. Outside, the pigeons on the roof were picking at each other, presumably removing insects. Perhaps this is all that we as human beings can do for each other, Letty thought. It was common knowledge that Marcia had recently had a serious operation. She was not a whole woman; some vital part of her had been taken away, though whether womb or breast was not generally known, Marcia herself revealing only that she had undergone 'major surgery'. But Letty did know that Marcia had had a breast removed, though even she did not know which one. Edwin and Norman had speculated on the matter and discussed it in the way men did; they felt that Marcia ought to have told them about it, seeing that they all worked together so closely. They could only conclude that the operation had made her even more peculiar than she had been already.

In the past both Letty and Marcia might have loved and been loved, but now the feeling that should have been directed towards husband, lover, child or even grandchild, had no natural outlet; no cat, dog, no bird, even, shared their lives and neither Edwin nor Norman had inspired love. Marcia had once had a cat but old Snowy had long since died, 'passed on' or 'been taken', however one liked to put it. In such circumstances women may feel a certain unsentimental tenderness towards each other, expressed in small gestures of solicitude, not unlike the pigeons picking insects off each other. Marcia, if she felt the need for such an outlet, was incapable of putting it into words. It was Letty who said, 'You look tired – shall I make you a cup of tea?' And when Marcia refused the offer, she went on, 'I hope your train won't be too crowded, that you'll get a seat – it should be better now, getting on for six o'clock.' She tried to smile at her, but when she looked at Marcia she saw that her dark eyes were alarmingly magnified behind her glasses, like the eyes of some nocturnal tree-climbing animal. A lemur or a potto, was it? Marcia, glancing sharply at Letty, thought, she's like an old sheep, but she means well even if she seems a bit interfering at times.

Norman, speeding northwards on the Stanmore branch of the Bakerloo line, was going to visit his brother-in-law in hospital. Now that his sister was dead there was no direct link between him and Ken, and Norman felt pleasantly virtuous at going to see him. He has no one, he thought, for the only child of the marriage had emigrated to New Zealand. In fact Ken did have somebody, a woman friend whom he expected to marry, but she did not visit on the same day as Norman. 'Let him come on his own,' they had said to each other, 'for after all he has no one and the visit will be a bit of company for him.'

Norman had never been in hospital himself but Marcia had dropped many hints about her experiences and especially about Mr Strong, the surgeon who had cut her up. Not that Ken's experience could be compared with hers but it gave one an idea. Norman was ready to surge through the swing doors with the crowd into the ward when the signal was given. He had not brought flowers or fruit, it being understood between them that the visit was all that was expected or required. Ken was not much of a one for reading either, though he was quite glad to glance at Norman's *Evening*

Standard. By profession he was a driving examiner and his present stay in hospital was the result, not of an accident with a middle-aged woman driver on test, as was jokingly assumed in the ward, but of a duodenal ulcer brought about by the worrying nature of life in general, to which the anxieties of his job must surely have contributed.

Norman sat down by the side of the bed, averting his eyes from the other patients. Ken seemed a bit low, he thought, but men did not look their best in bed. There was something very unattractive about the average man's pyjamas. The ladies made more of an effort with their pastel-coloured nighties and frilly bed jackets which Norman had caught glimpses of when he passed the women's medical ward on his way up. Ken's bedside table held only a box of paper handkerchiefs and a bottle of Lucozade beside the regulation plastic water jug and glass, but in the recess underneath Norman could see a metal bowl for vomiting and a curiously shaped 'vase' of a grey, cardboard-like material which he suspected was something to do with passing urine – waterworks, as he put it. The sight of these half-concealed objects made him feel uneasy and resentful, so that he didn't quite know what to say to his brother-in-law.

'Seems quiet tonight,' he remarked.

'The telly's broken down.'

'Oh, so that's it. I thought there was something different.' Norman glanced towards the centre table where the great box stood, its face now grey and silent as its viewers in their beds. It should have been covered with a cloth, if only for the sake of decency. 'When did this happen?'

'Yesterday, and they haven't done anything about it. You'd think it was the least they could do, wouldn't you?'

'Well, it'll give you more time for your thoughts,' said Norman, meaning to be sarcastic, even a little cruel, for what thoughts could Ken have better than telly? He could not have known that Ken did indeed have thoughts, dreams really, of the driving school he and his woman friend planned to set up together; how he lay thinking of names – something like 'Reliant' or 'Excelsior' was obviously suitable, then his fancy was suddenly arrested by the name 'Dolphin' and he had a vision of a fleet of cars, turquoise blue or buttercup yellow, swooping and gliding over the North Circular, never stalling at the traffic lights as learners so often did in real life. He thought too about the make of car they would have – nothing foreign or with the engine at the back – that seemed to be against nature, like a watch with a square face. He could not reveal any of this to Norman, who disliked the motor car and couldn't even drive one. Ken had always felt a sort of pitying contempt for him, being so unmanly and working as a clerk in an office with middle-aged women.

They sat almost in silence and it was a relief to both of them when the bell went and the visit was at an end.

'Everything all right?' Norman asked, now eagerly on his feet.

'The tea's too strong.'

'Oh,' Norman was nonplussed. As if he could do anything about a thing like that! What did Ken expect? 'Couldn't you ask Sister or one of the nurses to make it weaker or put more milk in it?'

'You'd still taste the strength, even so. It's strong to begin with, you see. Anyway I couldn't ask Sister or one of the nurses – it's not their job.'

'Well, the lady that makes the tea, then.'

'Catch me doing that,' said Ken obscurely. 'But strong tea's the last thing I should have with my complaint.' Norman shook himself like a tetchy little dog. He hadn't come here to be involved in this sort of thing, and he allowed himself to be hustled away by a bossy Irish nurse, with never a backward glance at the patient in the bed.

Outside, his irritable mood was intensified by the cars that rushed past, preventing him from crossing the road to the bus stop. Then he had to wait a long time for a bus and when he reached the square where he lived there were more cars, parked side by side, overlapping on to the pavement. Some of them were so large that their hindquarters – rumps, buttocks and bums – jutted over the kerb and he had to step aside to avoid them. 'Bugger,' he muttered, kicking one of them with a small ineffectual foot. 'Bugger, bugger, bugger.'

Nobody heard him. The almond trees were in flower but he did not see them and was unconscious of their blossom shining in the lamplight. He entered his front door and went into his bed-sitting room. The evening had exhausted him and he did not even feel that he had done Ken much good.

Edwin had spent a much more satisfactory evening. The attendance at the sung Mass had been pretty much as usual for a weekday – only seven in the congregation but the full complement in the sanctuary. Afterwards he and Father G. had gone to the pub for a drink. They had talked church shop – whether to order a stronger brand of incense now that the Rosa Mystica was nearly finished – should they let the young people organize the occasional Sunday evening service with guitars and that – what would be the reaction of the congregation if Father G. tried to introduce Series Three?

'All that standing up to pray,' Edwin said. 'People wouldn't like that.'

'But the Kiss of Peace – turning to the person next to you with a friendly gesture, rather a . . .' Father G. had been going to say 'beautiful idea', but perhaps, given his particular congregation, it wasn't quite the word.

Remembering the emptiness of the church at the service they had just attended, Edwin was also doubtful – not more than half a dozen dotted among the echoing pews and nobody standing next to anybody to make any kind of gesture – but he was too kind to spoil Father G.'s vision of a multitude of worshippers. He often thought regretfully of those days of the Anglo-Catholic revival in the last century and even the more sympathetic climate of twenty years ago, where Father G., tall and cadaverous in cloak and biretta, would have been rather more in place than in the church of the nineteen seventies where so many of the younger priests went in for jeans and long hair. One such had been in the pub that evening. Edwin's heart sank as he visualized the kind of services at *his* church. 'I think perhaps we'd better keep the evening service as it is,' he said, thinking dramatically, over my dead body, seeing himself trampled down by a horde of boys and girls brandishing guitars . . .

They parted outside Edwin's neat semi-detached house in a street not far from the common. Standing by the hatstand in the hall, Edwin was reminded of his dead wife, Phyllis. It was the moment of waiting outside the sitting room door before going in that brought her into his mind. He could almost hear her voice, a little querulous, asking, 'Is that you, Edwin?' As if it could be anybody else! Now he had all the freedom that loneliness brings – he could go to church as often as he liked, attend meetings that went on all evening, store stuff for jumble sales in the back room and leave it there for months. He could go to the pub or the vicarage and stay there till all hours.

Edwin went upstairs to bed humming a favourite Office Hymn, 'O Blest Creator of the Light'. It was tricky, the plainsong tune, and his efforts to get it right diverted his attention from the words. In any case it would be going a bit far to regard tonight's congregation as 'sunk in sin and whelmed with strife', as one line of the hymn put it. People nowadays wouldn't stand for that kind of talk. Perhaps that was one reason why so few went to church.

Two

SO OFTEN NOW Letty came upon reminders of her own mortality or, regarded less poetically, the different stages towards death. Less obvious than the obituaries in *The Times* and the *Telegraph* were what she thought of as 'upsetting' sights. This morning, for instance, a woman, slumped on a seat on the Underground platform while the rush hour crowds hurried past her, reminded her so much of a school contemporary that she forced herself to look back, to make quite sure that it was *not* Janet Belling. It appeared not to be, yet it could have been, and even if it wasn't it was still somebody, some woman driven to the point where she could find herself in this situation. Ought one to *do* anything? While Letty hesitated, a young woman, wearing a long dusty black skirt and shabby boots, bent over the slumped figure with a softly spoken enquiry. At once the figure reared itself up and shouted in a loud, dangerously uncontrolled voice, 'Fuck off!' Then it couldn't be Janet Belling, Letty thought, her first feeling one of relief; Janet would never have used such an expression. But fifty years ago nobody did – things were different now, so that was nothing to go by. In the meantime, the girl moved away with dignity. She had been braver than Letty.

*

That morning was a flag day. Marcia peered at the young woman standing with her tray and rattling tin outside the station. Something to do with cancer. Marcia advanced, quietly triumphant, a 10p coin in her hand.

The smiling girl was ready, the flag in the form of a little shield poised to stab into the lapel of Marcia's coat.

'Thank you,' she said, as the coin clattered down into the tin.

'A *very* good cause,' Marcia murmured, 'and one very dear to *me*. You see, I too have had...'

The girl waited nervously, her smile fading, but like Letty she was hypnotized by the marmoset eyes behind the thick glasses. And now promising young men who might have been induced to buy flags were slinking by into the station, pretending to be in a hurry.

'I, too,' Marcia repeated, 'have had *something removed*.'

At that moment an older man, attracted by the sight of the pretty flag-seller, approached and cut short Marcia's attempt at conversation, but the memory of her stay in hospital lasted her all the way to the office.

Marcia had been one of those women, encouraged by her mother, who had sworn that she would never let the surgeon's knife touch her body, a woman's body being such a private thing. But of course when it came to the point there was no question of resistance. She smiled as she remembered Mr Strong, the consultant surgeon who had performed the operation – mastectomy, hysterectomy, appendectomy, tonsillectomy – you name it, it was all one to him, his cool competent manner seemed to imply. She recalled his procession down the ward, surrounded by satellites, her eager observation and anticipation until the great moment when he arrived at her bed and she heard him ask, 'And how's Miss Ivory this morning?' in that almost teasing way. Then she would tell him how she was and he would listen, occasionally asking a question or turning to Sister for her opinion, the rather flippant manner replaced by professional concern.

If the surgeon was God, the chaplains were his ministers, a little lower than the housemen. The good-looking young Roman Catholic had come first, saying how we all needed a rest at times, though he did not look as if he could possibly need such a thing, and how being in hospital, unpleasant though it was in many ways, could sometimes prove to be a blessing in disguise, for there was no situation that couldn't be turned to good, and truly you could say that every cloud had a silver lining . . . He went on in this vein with such a flow of Irish charm that it was some time before Marcia could get in a word to tell him that she was not a Roman Catholic.

'Ah, then you'll be a Protestant.' The violence of the word had a stunning effect, as it must to anyone used to the vaguer and gentler 'Anglican' or 'Church of England'. 'Well, it's nice to have had this chat,' he conceded. 'The Protestant chaplain will be along to see you.'

The Anglican chaplain offered her Holy Communion and although she was not a practising churchwoman Marcia accepted, partly out of superstition but also because it gave her a kind of distinction in the ward. Only one other woman received the ministrations of the chaplain. The other patients criticized his crumpled surplice and wondered why he didn't get a nylon or terylene one, and recalled their own vicars refusing to marry people in their churches or to christen kiddies because their parents didn't go to church, and other such instances of unreasonable and unChristian behaviour.

Of course in hospital, and particularly when the chaplain visited her, the question of death did come into one's mind, and Marcia had asked herself the brutal question, if she were to die, having no close relatives, would it matter? She could be buried in a pauper's grave, if such a thing still existed, though she would leave money enough for a funeral; but her body could be shovelled into a furnace, she would never know. Might as well be realistic. Of course she could donate certain organs to assist in research or spare-part surgery. This last idea had an irresistible appeal, linked as it was with the thought of Mr Strong, and she meant to fill in the form at the back of the booklet they had given her when she entered the hospital. But in the end she never got round to it and anyway her operation had been a success and she had *not* died. 'I shall not die but live' – there had been a poem that came into her mind at the time. She didn't read poetry now, or anything else for that matter, but sometimes she remembered the odd tag.

As she waited on the platform that morning Marcia noticed that somebody had scrawled in crude capital letters, KILL ASIAN SHIT. She stared at the inscription and mouthed the words to herself as if considering their implication. They brought back another hospital memory, of a man who had wheeled her on the trolley to the operating theatre, bearded and with a remote, dignified beauty, his head and body swathed in bluish gauze. He had called her 'dear'.

The three others looked up as Marcia entered the room.

'Late, aren't you?' Norman snapped.

As if it had anything to do with him, Letty thought. 'There's been some delay on the Underground this morning,' she said.

'Oh, yes,' Norman agreed. 'Did you see that on the blackboard at Holborn station? Trains were delayed "due to a person under the train at Hammersmith", it said. A "person" – is that what you have to say now?'

'Poor soul,' said Edwin. 'One does wonder sometimes how these tragedies occur.'

Letty was silent, remembering her own upsetting experience. That woman might find herself under a train one day. She had not mentioned it before but now she did.

'Dear me,' said Norman, 'that looks like a good example of somebody who's fallen through the net of the welfare state.'

'It could happen to anyone,' said Letty, 'but there's really no need for anyone nowadays to get into that sort of state.' She glanced down at her tweed skirt, old but newly cleaned and pressed; at least one could keep up reasonable standards.

Marcia said nothing, but stared in her disconcerting way.

Norman said almost chirpily, 'Oh, well, that's another thing we've all got coming to us, or at least the possibility – falling through the net of the welfare state.'

'Don't keep on about it,' said Edwin. 'What with being found dead of hypothermia, you seem to've got it on the brain.'

'Dead of starvation's more likely,' said Norman. He had been to the supermarket on his way to work and now proceeded to check the items in his shopping bag – a 'psychedelic' plastic carrier, patterned in vivid colours, hinting at some unexpected aspect of his character – against the printed slip he had received at the check-out. 'Crispbread 16, tea 18, cheese 34, butter beans, the small tin, 12,' he recited. 'Bacon 46, but that was the smallest pack I could find, smoked oyster back, they called it, not really the best. You'd think they'd do it up smaller for people living alone, wouldn't you. The woman in front of me spent over twelve pounds – just my luck to get behind somebody like that at the check-out,' he droned on.

'I should put the bacon in a cooler place if I were you,' said Letty.

'Yes, I'll pop it in one of the filing cabinets,' said Norman. 'Don't let me forget it. You read of elderly people being found dead in the house with no food – dreadful, isn't it?'

'There's no need for that,' said Edwin.

'It is possible to store tins,' said Marcia, in a remote sort of way.

'But then you might not have the strength to open them,' said Norman with relish. 'Anyway, I don't have much storage space.'

Marcia glanced at him thoughtfully. She wondered sometimes about Norman's domestic arrangements but of course nobody had ever seen his bed-sitting room. The four who worked together did not visit each other or meet after office hours. When she had first come here, Marcia had experienced a faint stirring of interest in Norman, a feeling that was a good many degrees cooler than tenderness but which nevertheless occupied her thoughts briefly. Once at lunchtime she had followed him. At a safe distance behind, she had watched him as he picked his way through the fallen leaves and called out angrily after a car which had failed to stop at a zebra crossing. She found herself entering the British Museum, ascending wide stone steps and walking through echoing galleries filled with alarming images and objects in glass cases, until they came to rest in the Egyptian section by a display of mummified animals and small crocodiles. Here Norman had mingled with a crowd of school children and Marcia slipped away. If she had thought of making herself known to him, the time and such questions as 'Do you come here often?' were obviously inappropriate. Norman had not revealed to any of them that he visited the British Museum, and even if he had would never have admitted to the contemplation of mummified crocodiles. No doubt it was a secret thing. As time went on Marcia's feeling for Norman waned. Then she went into hospital and Mr Strong entered her life and filled her thoughts. Now she hardly considered Norman at all, except as a rather silly little man, so his fussing with his shopping and his reading out the things he had bought only irritated her. She did not want to know what he was going to eat – it was of no interest whatsoever.

'That reminds me, I must get a loaf at lunchtime,' said Edwin. 'Father G.'s coming in for a bite before the PCC meeting and I'll do one of my specials – baked beans on toast with a poached egg on top.'

The women smiled, as they were meant to, but Edwin was known to be a competent cook and it was not as if they had anything much grander for their own evening meals, he thought, as he came out of a teashop that sold bread, carrying a large white loaf wrapped in a paper bag. He had had a light lunch, snack really, in the teashop whose decor had changed distressingly, though the food was the same. Edwin and the other regular patrons felt themselves out of place among so much trendy orange and olive green and imitation stripped pine. There were hanging lights and shades patterned with butterflies and over it all soft 'muzak', difficult to hear but insidious. Edwin didn't like change, and now that Gamage's had been pulled down it was a relief to do his lunchtime church crawl, though even the Church, the dear old C of E, was not immune to change. Sometimes he would slip in for a prayer or a look round and a read of the parish magazine if there was one, but mostly he studied the noticeboards to see what was offered in the way of services and other activities. Today he was attracted by the announcement of an austerity luncheon in aid of a well-known charity, but rather surprisingly 'with wine' – that might be worth a visit.

Letty did her shopping on the way home, at a small self-service store run by Uganda Asians that stayed open till eight o'clock in the evening. She bought only tinned or packaged foods, feeling a doubt about anything exposed to the air. In her comfortable bed-sitting room, which had a washbasin behind a screen and a small electric cooker, she prepared a meal of rice with the remains of a chicken, then settled herself to listen to the wireless and continue working on a tapestry chair-seat she was making.

The house belonged to an elderly woman who took in, as the most refined type of lodgers, two others like herself and a

Hungarian refugee, who had more or less adapted herself to the ways of the house – one's radio considerately turned down and the bathroom left as one would wish to find it. It was a comfortable enough life, if a little sterile, perhaps even deprived. But deprivation implied once having had something to be deprived of, like Marcia's breast, to give a practical example, and Letty had never really had anything much. Yet, she sometimes wondered, might not the experience of 'not having' be regarded as something with its own validity?

There was a play on the radio that evening, going backwards into the life of an old woman. It reminded Letty of the woman she had seen slumped on the seat on the Underground platform that morning, as if one might visualize her this time last year, say, then five years ago, ten years, twenty, thirty, even forty. But this kind of going back was hardly for Letty herself, who lived very much in the present, holding neatly and firmly on to life, coping as best she could with whatever it had to offer, little though that might be. Her curriculum vitae presented the kind of reading of so many like herself born before 1914, the only child of middle-class parents. She had arrived in London in the late twenties to take a secretarial course, staying in a working-girls' hostel where she had met her friend Marjorie, the only person she still kept up with from those far-off days. Like most girls of her generation and upbringing she had expected to marry, and when the war came there were great opportunities for girls to get a man or form an attachment, even with a married man, but Marjorie had been the one to marry, leaving Letty in her usual position of trailing behind her friend. By the end of the war Letty was over thirty and Marjorie had given up hope for her. Letty had never had much hope anyway. The immediate post-war years were fixed in her memory by the clothes she had worn on particular dates – the New Look brought in by Dior in 1947, the comfortable elegance of the fifties, and in the early sixties the horror of the mini-skirt, such a cruel fashion for those no longer young. And only the other day Letty had walked past the building in Bloomsbury where she and Marjorie had worked in the thirties – it had been on the first floor of a Georgian house – and found herself facing a concrete structure. Rather like the building where she now worked with the other three, but of course she never noticed that.

That night, as if inspired by the radio play, Letty had a dream. She was back at the time of the Silver Jubilee, staying with Marjorie and her fiancé Brian in the country cottage they had bought for £300. There was a friend of Brian's there too, intended for Letty, a handsome but dull young man called Stephen. On the Saturday evening they went to the pub and sat in the quiet musty saloon bar with its mahogany furniture and stuffed fish. It felt damp as if nobody ever used it, as indeed nobody did except timid visitors like themselves. They all had beer, though the girls didn't like it much and it seemed to have no noticeable 'effect' on them, except to make them wonder whether there was a ladies' cloakroom in such a primitive place. On the other side, in the public bar, there was light and colour and noise, but they, the four young people, were outside it all. On Sunday they went to Matins at the village church. There were bird-droppings on the altar and the vicar appealed for donations towards the repair of the roof. In 1970 the church was closed as redundant and the building was eventually pulled down as being of no architectural or historical interest. In Letty's dream she was lying in the long grass with Stephen, or somebody vaguely like him, in that hot summer of 1935. He was very near to her, but nothing happened. She did not know what had become of Stephen but Marjorie was a widow now, as alone as Letty in her bedsitter. All gone, that time, those people ... Letty woke up and lay for some time meditating on the strangeness of life, slipping away like this.

Three

MARCIA ENTERED HER house, that house which, in the estate agents' language, was on its way to becoming a 'twenty-thousand semi'. Houses in that road were already reaching nearly that figure but Marcia's house was not quite like the others. From the outside it looked ordinary enough, with stained-glass panels in the front door, two large bow windows and a smaller window over the porch. The outside paint was a conventional dark green and cream, now in need of re-doing, and the net curtains at the windows could have done with a wash, some thought. But Miss Ivory went out to work and she was not the sort of person you could offer to help. Her neighbours in the more fashionably done-up houses on either side were newcomers. They sometimes passed the time of day with her but Marcia had not been into their houses nor they into hers.

Inside, the house was dark with brown-painted doors kept mysteriously closed. Dust lay everywhere. Marcia went straight through to the kitchen where she deposited her shopping bag on the newspaper-covered table. She knew that she ought to start getting a meal. The almoner, or medical social worker as they called it now, at the hospital had said how important it was for the working woman to have a good meal when she came home in the evening, but all Marcia did was to fill the kettle for a cup of tea. Her energies had already been spent that morning preparing her lunch to eat in the office. She could not think of any other kind of food now though she might have a biscuit with her tea. 'Biscuits keep you going,' they used to say in the war, but she had never had a big appetite. She had always been thin and since being in hospital she had become even thinner. Her clothes hung loosely on her but she didn't really care how she looked, not like Letty who was always buying new things and worried if she couldn't get a cardigan in the exact shade to match something.

Suddenly a bell rang, shrill and peremptory. Marcia was as if frozen into her chair. She never had visitors and nobody ever called. Who could it be, and in the evening? The bell rang again and she got up and went into the front room where from a side window she could see who was standing on the doorstep.

It was a young woman, swinging a bunch of car keys in her hand. Marcia could see a small blue car parked on the opposite side of the road. Reluctantly she opened the door.

'Ah, Miss Ivory, isn't it? I'm Janice Brabner.'

She had a rather pink, open face. Young women nowadays didn't seem to bother much with make-up and even Marcia could see that some would have been improved by it.

'Some of us at the Centre have been worrying about the lonely ones.'

Could she really have prepared that sentence, for this was what came out. Marcia gave her no encouragement.

'I mean, the people who live alone.'

'Did you think I might be found dead? Was that the idea?'

'Oh, Miss Ivory, of course we had nothing like that in mind!'

It seemed to be almost an occasion for laughter but Janice Brabner was sure this couldn't be right. Doing voluntary work at the Centre wasn't exactly funny even if one smiled sometimes at the people one visited, for some of them were rather sweet. But they could be tragic. Miss Ivory, for instance, in what category should she be placed? It was known that her mother had died some years ago, that she now lived alone and that she had recently left hospital after a major operation. The medical social worker, whom Janice knew, had dropped a hint, suggested that it might be as well to keep an eye on her. It was true that she went out to work but nobody seemed to know much about her – she didn't speak to neighbours and nobody had ever been into her house. She did not invite Janice to come in now and they continued their conversation on the doorstep. Of course one couldn't force one's way into people's houses, but surely a lonely person like Miss Ivory would welcome a friendly advance and a chat?

'We just wondered,' Janice went on, realizing the need for tact and caution, as she had been instructed, 'if you'd like to come along to a get-together at the Centre one evening. It's next to the town hall, you know.'

'I don't think so,' said Marcia firmly. 'I go out to work and my evenings are fully occupied.'

But there was no television aerial on the house, so what did she do in the evenings? Janice wondered. Still, she had done all she could, sown a seed, perhaps; that was the main thing.

No sooner was the door closed than Marcia went up to the front bedroom to watch Janice Brabner go. She saw her unlock her car and then sit in it with a list in her hand which she appeared to be consulting. Then she drove away.

Marcia turned back into the room where her mother had died. It had been left almost untouched since then. Of course the body had been removed and buried, all that was necessary in that way had been done and the proper obsequies performed, but after that Marcia had lacked the energy to rearrange the furniture and Mrs Williams, the woman who came in to clean at that time, had not encouraged her. 'You want to remember things as they were, not go changing them,' she had said. She did not care for moving furniture, anyway. The bed had become the place where the cat Snowy slept until his death, when the black part of his fur had taken on a brownish tinge and his body had become light, until one day, in the fullness of time, he had ceased to breathe, a peaceful end. He was twenty years old, one hundred and forty in human terms. 'You wouldn't want to be that old,' Mrs Williams had said, as if one had the choice or could do anything about it. After Snowy's death and burial in the garden, Mrs Williams had left, the work having become too much for her, and Marcia made no pretence of doing anything to the room. On the bed cover there was still an old fur ball, brought up by Snowy in his last days, now dried up like some ancient mummified relic of long ago.

'Miss Ivory has funny staring eyes. And she obviously didn't want to ask me in,' said Janice, back at the Centre, basking now in the relief of an awkward duty done.

'Oh, you mustn't let that put you off,' said an older and more experienced colleague. 'A lot of them seem like that at first, but the contact has been made, that's the chief thing. And that's what we have to do – *make contact*, by force, if necessary. Believe me, it can be *most* rewarding.'

Janice wondered about this, but said nothing.

Over the other side of the common Edwin, on an evening walk, was studying a church noticeboard. It offered nothing but the barest essentials – Holy Communion at eight on Sundays, Matins at eleven, no weekday services – and when he turned the handle of the door he found that it was locked. A pity, but that was the way things were now – it wasn't safe to leave a church open, what with thefts and vandalism. With a slight feeling of frustration he turned away and began walking along the road until he reached a side turning which seemed to go in the direction he wanted. Then he read the name of the road and realized that it was where Marcia lived and he walked on quickly. It would be embarrassing to meet her, even to walk past her house, he felt. They were both, in a sense, lonely people but neither would have expected to meet the other outside office hours. Any kind of encounter would fill her with a dismay equal to his. In any case, Edwin always felt that Norman was more Marcia's friend than he was, more her cup of tea if anyone was. Was he, Edwin, then Letty's friend? Well, hardly that. Something in the idea made him smile and he walked away along the common, a tall, smiling figure carrying a raincoat, although it was a warm evening and the sky was cloudless.

Four

WITH THE COMING of spring, merging into the sunshine of early May, there was a subtle change in the lunchtime occupations of the four in the office. Edwin went on his usual church crawl, for that season of the year was stiff with festivals and the churches in the area had a rich and varied programme to offer, but he also frequented gardening shops and called at travel agents and collected brochures with the possibility of arranging a late holiday, everyone else having booked theirs in January. Norman plucked up his courage to visit the dentist and arrived at the office feeling very sorry for himself, and with a Thermos of soup which was all he could manage for his lunch.

Marcia forsook the public library and wandered into a shop full of loud music, merchandise from foreign parts and badly finished eastern-style garments for both sexes. She fingered the crude pottery and the garish flimsy blouses and skirts but did not buy anything. The almost deafening pop music confused her and she felt that people were staring at her. She went out into the sunshine, dazed and bewildered. Then she was roused into alertness by the clang of an ambulance bell and she found herself joining a knot of people gathered round a slumped figure on the pavement. Somebody had collapsed with a coronary, a window cleaner had slipped and fallen – the air was full of excited, confused murmurings, but nobody quite knew what had happened. Marcia attached herself to two women and tried to find out, but all they could say was, 'Poor soul, doesn't he look terrible – what a shock for his wife.' Her thoughts went back to her own stay in hospital and the excitement when an ambulance came in, for she had been in a ground-floor ward very near Casualty. It was rather disappointing now to see the man on the pavement attempting to get up, but the ambulance men restrained him and bundled him in and Marcia, a smile on her lips, went back to the office.

Norman and Letty both felt the pull of the open air, Norman to take his mind off his teeth, and Letty because she had the slightly obsessive or cranky idea that one ought to get a walk of some kind every day. So they both made their way, separately and unaware of each other, to Lincoln's Inn Fields, the nearest open space to the office.

Norman gravitated towards the girls playing netball and sat down uneasily. He could not analyse the impulse that had brought him there, an angry little man whose teeth hurt – angry at the older men who, like himself, formed the majority of the spectators round the netball pitch, angry at the semi-nudity of the long-haired boys and girls lying on the grass, angry at the people sitting on seats eating sandwiches or sucking ice lollies and cornets and throwing the remains on the ground. As he watched the netball girls, leaping and cavorting in their play, the word 'lechery' came into his head and something about 'grinning like a dog', a phrase in the psalms, was it; then he thought of the way some dogs did appear to grin, their tongues lolling out. After a few minutes' watching he got up and made his way back to the office, dissatisfied with life. Only the sight of a wrecked motor car, with one side all bashed in, being towed up Kingsway by a breakdown van, gave him the kind of lift Marcia had experienced on hearing the bell of the ambulance, but then he remembered that an abandoned car had been parked outside the house where he lived for some days, and the police or the council ought to do something about it, and that made him angry again.

Letty, with her feelings on the subject of exercise and fresh air, was prepared to enjoy these amenities.

One impulse from a vernal wood
May teach you more of man,
Of moral evil and of good,
Than all the sages can.

She knew all about that, even if she was not prepared to go too deeply into the implications of those lines. She walked briskly and did not think of sitting down, for most of the seats were occupied and those that had space contained obvious eccentrics, muttering to themselves and eating strange things. It was better to go on walking, though it was hot and she would have liked a rest. Letty was not angry when she saw the young people kissing and cuddling on the grass, even if such behaviour was different from that of forty years ago when she was a girl. But was it so different? Or could it be that she had not noticed such things in those days? She passed a building concerned with Cancer Research and she thought of Marcia. Even Marcia had once hinted at something in her own life, long ago. No doubt everybody had once had something in their lives? Certainly it was the kind of thing people liked to imply, making one suspect that a good deal was being made out of almost nothing.

Back in the office the talk was about holidays. Edwin's brochures advertising impossible delights had been spread out on his table for some weeks now, but it was known that he never did more than leaf through their pages, for his annual holiday was invariably spent with his daughter and her family.

'Greece,' said Norman, taking up a booklet with a picture of the Acropolis on the cover. 'I've always had a fancy to go there.'

Marcia looked up, startled. The others were surprised too but did not show it. What was this? What new aspect of Norman's life, what never before expressed longing was to be revealed? His holidays, always taken in England, were usually characterized by disaster.

'They say it's the wonderful light, a special quality it has,' said Letty, repeating something she had once heard or read. 'And the wine-dark sea – isn't that how it's described?'

'Oh, I don't care what colour the sea is,' said Norman. 'It's the swimming that would attract me.'

'You mean skin diving and that sort of thing?' said Edwin in astonishment.

'Why not?' Norman was defiant. 'Lots of people do it, you know. They find buried treasure and that.'

Edwin began to laugh. 'It would be a bit different from that holiday of yours last year,' he joked. Norman had been on a coach trip to the West Country when, for some unspecified reason, his only comment had been 'Never again.' 'I shouldn't think you found much buried treasure *there.*'

'I can never understand why people have to leave their homes the way they do,' said Marcia. 'When you're older you don't really need holidays.' If Norman really had these secret longings it ought to be enough for him to go and sit in the British Museum at lunchtime, contemplating the riches of vanished civilizations, she felt. Marcia herself never went away; her absences from the office were spent in mysterious ploys of her own.

'Oh, well, looking at the pictures is probably as far as I'll get,' said Norman. 'Not like Letty here.'

'I've never been to Greece,' said Letty, but she was by far the most adventurous of the four of them. She had been on several package tours abroad with Marjorie, and her postcards of Spain,

Italy and Yugoslavia still brightened the office walls. But this year Marjorie seemed to want to stay at home and as Letty was going to share her cottage with her when she retired it seemed quite a good idea for her to get used to living in the country. During her fortnight Letty would be getting a taste of village life, with excursions to the surrounding country and picnic lunches when the weather permitted. 'Roses round the door and all that,' as Norman used to say when Letty's retirement plans were mentioned. 'But of course the weather can spoil things,' he couldn't resist adding. 'Don't I know!'

Five

A PHEASANT SAT in the middle of a field, unconcerned as the train drew into the platform. Letty could see Marjorie's dusty blue Morris 1000 standing among the larger and sleeker cars parked at the station. Even now, forty years later, she was reminded of 'Beelzebub', Marjorie's first car bought for £25 in the nineteen thirties. Did young people still give their old cars facetious names, Letty wondered. Motoring was a much more serious business now, hardly fun at all, when the car was an important status symbol and large sums of money could be paid for particularly desirable registration numbers.

Marjorie seized Letty's bag and stuffed it into the boot. As a comfortable widow living in the country, she seemed far removed from the dashing young woman that Letty remembered from their earlier days, even if she still retained some romantic extravagances. Now she seemed rather excessively interested in the new vicar who had recently been appointed and Letty saw him for the first time when – surprisingly for Marjorie – she insisted on taking her to church on Sunday morning. The Reverend David Lydell (he liked to be called 'Father') was a tall dark man in his middle forties who certainly looked good in his vestments. Nice for Marjorie to have an interesting new vicar, Letty thought, generously indulgent. Most of the inhabitants of the village were retired married couples with the ritual grandchildren. There was a certain amount of formal social life, mostly consisting of the drinking of sherry at certain times, and one evening Marjorie invited an elegant retired colonel, who had no conversation, and his wife, who had a good deal more, and Father Lydell, in for a drink. Seen at closer quarters and in 'civilian' clothes, Father Lydell was disappointing. He looked sadly ordinary in a ginger-coloured tweed jacket and grey flannel trousers with something not quite right about the cut of them – too wide or too narrow, or at least not what one saw people wearing now.

After a decent interval and a couple of glasses each, the colonel and his wife left, but Father Lydell, obviously with no evening meal of his own in view, lingered on, so that Marjorie had to ask him to stay to supper.

'One is at a slight disadvantage,' he said elliptically, when Marjorie left the room to prepare the meal and he and Letty were left alone.

'Oh? In what way?' Letty was not sure whether he meant the disadvantage to apply to himself or to the human race in general.

'In being unable to return hospitality,' he explained. 'Marjorie has been so kind.'

So he called her by her Christian name, and there had been other meals.

'I think people in a village usually are hospitable,' said Letty, diminishing him a little. 'More so than in London.'

'Ah, *London* . . .' Was the sigh too extravagant?

'Of course David is here for his health,' said Marjorie, coming back into the room and entering eagerly into the conversation.

'Do you find the country is doing you good?' Letty asked.

'I've had diarrhoea all this week,' came the disconcerting reply.

There was a momentary – perhaps no more than a split second's – pause, but if the women had been temporarily taken aback, they were by no means at a loss.

'Diarrhoea,' Letty repeated, in a clear, thoughtful tone. She was never certain how to spell the word, but felt that such a trivial admission was lacking in proper seriousness so she said no more.

'Strong drink would do you more good than the eternal parish cups of tea,' Marjorie suggested boldly. 'Brandy, perhaps.'

'Enterovioform,' said Letty.

He smiled pityingly. 'All those English on package tours on the Costa Brava may find it helpful, but my case is rather different . . .'

The sentence trailed off, leaving the difference to be imagined.

'Well, when one *is* abroad . . . When we were in Naples, *Napoli*,' said Marjorie, almost roguishly. 'Do you remember that time in Sorrento, Letty?'

'I only remember the lemon groves,' said Letty, determined to change the subject.

David Lydell closed his eyes and lay back in his chair, thinking how agreeable it was to be in the company of gentlewomen. Far more what he was accustomed to. The rough voices of the village people grated on his nerves and sometimes they said cruel things. Any attempts he had made to 'improve' the church services had met with scorn and hostility and when he tried to visit the cottages he was forced to look at television programmes which they hadn't even the good manners to turn off. He found it shocking that such people should have no running water or indoor sanitation and yet be slaves to the box. Even the old women, who might have been the backbone of the congregation in earlier times, seemed disinclined to attend church, even if conveyed there and back by car. The only services that drew congregations of any size were Harvest Festival, Remembrance Sunday and the Carol Service at Christmas. By contrast, Marjorie and her friend, Miss Something, a not very interesting person whose name he hadn't caught, were highly civilized and he enjoyed eating *poulet niçoise* and talking about holidays in France and Italy.

'Orvieto,' he murmured. 'Of course one wants to drink it *there*,' and naturally they agreed with him.

Letty thought him rather tiresome but she did not say as much to Marjorie. The weather was good and she did not want to raise controversial subjects over tea in the garden or during leisurely country walks. Besides, if she was going to share Marjorie's cottage in her retirement it would be as well not to be too critical of the vicar, especially as it seemed that he might often be dropping in. That was one of the country things she would have to get used to. There were other things too. On their walks she was always the one to find the dead bird and the dried-up hedgehog's body or to notice the mangled rabbit in the middle of the road when they were driving. She supposed that Marjorie had seen them so often that she no longer found them upsetting.

On the last day of Letty's holiday they were to go for a picnic to a nearby beauty spot. As it was a weekday the place would be less crowded and, best of all, as Marjorie revealed just before they started out, David Lydell would be able to accompany them.

'But won't he have things to do during the week?' Letty protested. 'Even if there aren't any services, doesn't he have to visit the sick and the old people?'

'There's only one sick person at the moment and he's in hospital, and the old people don't want visits from the clergy,' said Marjorie, making Letty realize that it was no good thinking that such old-fashioned notions could be applied in these days of the welfare state or in a village where the health of every person was known and commented on. 'I try to get David out into the countryside as much as I can,' Marjorie added. 'He needs to get right away and relax.'

Letty noted the use of the term 'countryside', which seemed to have a special significance, and bearing David Lydell's need in mind, she was not surprised to find herself squashed into the back of the car with the picnic things and Marjorie's old sealyham which left stiff white hairs all over Letty's neat navy-blue trousers. David and Marjorie in the front made conversation about village matters which Letty could not join in.

When they arrived at the picnic spot, Marjorie produced two folding canvas chairs from the boot of the car and these were solemnly put up for herself and David, Letty having quickly assured them that she would just as soon sit on the rug – indeed, she preferred it. All the same, she could not help feeling in some way belittled or diminished, sitting on a lower level than the others.

After they had eaten cold ham and hard-boiled eggs and drunk white wine – an unusual touch, this, which Letty could only attribute to the presence of David Lydell – the three of them fell silent; perhaps, because of drinking wine in the middle of the day, a natural desire for sleep overcame them. An awkward arrangement for sleeping – three people, two in the chairs and Letty down below – but she closed her eyes against her will and for a short time was unaware of her surroundings.

When she opened her eyes she found herself looking straight up at Marjorie and David, their canvas chairs pushed close together, apparently locked in an embrace.

Letty immediately looked away and closed her eyes again, wondering if she had been dreaming.

'More coffee anyone?' Marjorie asked in a bright tone. 'There's some in the other thermos. Letty, I think you've been asleep.'

Letty sat up, 'Yes, I think I must have dropped off,' she admitted. Had she imagined the whole scene, or was this another of the things she was going to have to get used to when she lived in the country?

No sooner had Letty come back from her holiday than Edwin went on his. There had been a good deal of discussion in the office as to whether he should go by coach or by train and the advantages and snags of each method were endlessly weighed up. In the end the train won. It was more expensive but it was quicker, and Edwin would get enough motoring with his son-in-law and daughter and the two children. They would be in easy reach of Eastbourne, where there were some splendid churches, and he was looking forward to that. In addition there would be visits to a safari park and to the stately homes that offered the best attractions; perhaps they would even go as far afield as the Lions of Longleat, driving on as many motorways as possible, the men in the front of the car, Edwin's daughter and the children in the back. It would be a break for all of them, but soon, with the children growing up, they might want to go to Spain, and then what was to be done about Edwin? He wouldn't like Spain, they decided. Perhaps he could go on holiday with one of the people from his office; that might be a solution to the problem.

Edwin hardly gave a thought to his working companions when he was away from them. It was only Marcia who came into his mind and that was in a rather curious way, when he was standing at the station bookstall before his train went, wondering whether he should buy something to read. He had already slipped down to Portugal Street to get that week's *Church Times* but that might not last him the whole journey. There was a colourful range of magazines on the counter, some of which displayed the full naked breasts of young women, enticingly posed. Edwin looked at them dispassionately. He supposed that his wife Phyllis had once had breasts but he could not remember that they had been at all like this, so very round and balloon-like. Then he recalled Marcia and her operation – mastectomy, he believed it was called, Norman had told him at the time. That meant that she had had a breast removed, a deprivation for any woman, though he could not imagine that Marcia had ever been endowed quite so abundantly as the girls on the magazine covers. Still, one must feel compassion for her even though she was not at all a lovable person. Perhaps he should have dropped in that evening he found himself over the other side of the common, passing the road where she lived. He wondered if she ever went to the church with the locked door, if the vicar ever called to see her. She had never mentioned it but no doubt somebody from that church was keeping an eye on her and knew that she was the kind of person who liked to keep herself to herself and must not be organized in any way. Although Edwin was not of the school that regarded the church as an extension of the social services, he knew very well that it was the attitude of a number of very good people nowadays, conscientious and well-meaning. It was very likely that Marcia would not be neglected, so there was no need to worry about her. There was certainly nothing he could do at this moment, standing on Victoria Station. So, turning away from the magazines that had reminded him of Marcia, he bought a copy of *Reader's Digest* and dismissed her from his thoughts.

The church people did make a mild effort with Marcia and suggested that she might like to join a coach trip to Westcliff-on-Sea ('Much nicer than Southend, dear'), but she didn't seem to want to go and of course they couldn't force her. Janice Brabner also was concerned that she didn't seem to be getting a holiday and made various suggestions, none of which met with Marcia's approval. 'She's so *difficult*,' Janice complained to her friend, who was a medical social worker. 'People like that don't seem to want to be helped. And yet some of them are so grateful, it's lovely, really, makes it all worth while . . .' she sighed. Marcia certainly wasn't like that.

Yet Marcia did have two holiday treats in store, though she had no intention of revealing to anybody what these were. The first was a visit to out-patients at the hospital, where she was due for a check-up at Mr Strong's clinic. The time indicated on her card was 11.35, a funny sort of time, giving the impression that the appointments were calculated so exactly to the nearest five minutes that there would be none of the usual hanging about. She arrived at the hospital punctually, checked in at the appointments desk and sat down to wait. If you were too early you could read a magazine or get a cup of tea or coffee out of the machine and of course there was always a visit to the toilet. Marcia did none of these things but sat staring in front of her. She had chosen a seat away from the other people and she was annoyed when a woman moved up next to her and appeared to want to get into conversation. The people waiting did not talk to each other; it was like the waiting room in a doctor's surgery except that there was something more sacred about the vigil here, each person having 'something wrong'. Marcia did not respond when a remark was made about the weather, but continued to stare straight in front of her, fixing her eyes on a door that had a notice over it saying 'Mr D.G. Strong'. Next to it was another door where the notice said 'Dr H. Wintergreen'. It was impossible to tell which of the people sitting in the chairs were waiting for the surgeon and which for the physician; there did not appear to be any distinguishing marks, for even though they all seemed to be rather cowed, some even broken, they were of both sexes and all ages.

'You waiting to see Dr Wintergreen?' Marcia's neighbour persisted.

'No,' said Marcia.

'Oh, then you must be for Mr Strong. Nobody's gone into *that* room for the last half hour, ever since I've been here. I'm waiting for Dr Wintergreen. He's a lovely doctor, foreign. I think he might be Polish. He's got ever such kind eyes, lovely. He always wore a carnation in his buttonhole when he came round the ward. He grows them himself, he's got a big house in Hendon. Digestive disorders, stomach, you know, that's his speciality and of course he's in Harley Street, too. Is Mr Strong in Harley Street?'

'Yes,' said Marcia coldly. She did not want to talk about Mr Strong, to discuss sacred matters with this person.

'Sometimes they get the Registrar to do the operation,' the

woman went on. 'Still, they've got to learn haven't they, how to do it . . . ?'

At that moment the nurse called out Marcia's name and she knew that her turn had come. She was not so naive as to imagine that Mr Strong's name on the door was a guarantee of his presence in the room, so she was not unduly cast down when, having half undressed and lain down on a couch, she was examined by a golden-haired boy, a houseman doing his training in surgery. He prodded her in a highly professional manner, took her blood pressure and listened with his stethoscope. Of course he did not notice her new pink underwear but did comment admiringly on the neatness of her operation scar – Mr Strong's work, of course – and told her that she was too thin and ought to eat more. Yet he, just coming up to his twenty-fifth birthday, hardly knew what to expect of a woman in her sixties. Were they always as thin as this? Certainly his great aunt, the nearest equivalent he could think of, was not at all like Miss Ivory, though he had never seen her without clothes.

'I think perhaps somebody should keep an eye on you,' he said kindly, and Marcia was not at all offended or irritated as she was when the social workers and the church people implied the same thing, for hospital was different. She was quietly triumphant when she handed her card in at the appointments desk to arrange for a further check-up at some future date.

Marcia's second holiday treat was a visit to Mr Strong's house, or rather to view at a safe distance the house where he lived. She knew from the telephone directory that he functioned not only in Harley Street but also at an address in Dulwich, a district easily reached by her on a 37 bus.

She let a week elapse after her visit to the hospital – spacing out the treats – before setting out on a fine afternoon to see Mr Strong's house. The bus was nearly empty and the conductress kind and helpful. She knew the best stop for the road Marcia asked for, but when she had punched the ticket she seemed, like the woman at the hospital, to want to chat. They were lovely houses in that road – did Marcia know somebody who lived there or – for this seemed unlikely – was she perhaps going after a job there? It was dreadful, Marcia felt, the way so many people wanted to know one's business and, when she did not respond, to tell one about their own. She had to listen to quite a long story about husband and kiddies, categories she knew nothing about, but at last the stop was reached and she got out and walked along the road in the sunshine.

The house was imposing, as were its neighbours, just the kind of house that looked worthy of Mr Strong. There were shrubs in the front garden. Marcia imagined the laburnum trees and the lilacs in May, but now in early August there wasn't much to admire. Perhaps there were roses at the back, for the garden behind the house seemed extensive, but all she could see was a swing hanging from a massive old tree. Of course Mr Strong was a family man; he had children, and now they were all away at the seaside. The house seemed completely deserted which meant that Marcia could stand in the road gazing, noticing discreetly drawn curtains in a William Morris design. It went through her mind that there were no net curtains here, they did not seem to go with Mr Strong. Her thoughts were unformulated, it was enough just to stand. Afterwards she waited for over half an hour at the bus stop, unconscious of the delay, time passing and no bus. Eventually she reached home and made a cup of tea and boiled an egg. The young doctor at the hospital had told her she ought to eat more and she was sure Mr Strong would agree with that.

Next day she returned to the office, but when they asked her how she had spent her leave she was evasive, only saying that the weather had been good and she'd had a nice break, which was what people always said.

*

The first day of Norman's leave was brilliantly sunny, the kind of day for going to the country or the seaside or for walking hand in hand with a lover in Kew Gardens.

None of these ideas occurred to Norman when he woke up and realized that he did not have to go to the office that day. As there was plenty of time, he decided to have a cooked breakfast – bacon and eggs with all the trimmings, which for him meant tomatoes and fried bread – far more than his usual plate of cornflakes or All-Bran. And he would have it in his pyjamas and dressing gown, just like somebody in a Noel Coward play. If they could see me now! he thought, meaning Edwin, Letty and Marcia.

The dressing gown was a jazzy rayon satin, patterned with a design of maroon and 'old gold' geometrical shapes. Norman had bought it at a sale, thinking he might look good in it, that it might in some unspecified way 'do' something for him. He was willing to bet that Edwin had nothing like this, probably just an old plaid woollen thing that he'd had since school days. He was pretty sure that Letty would have something smart, frilly and all the rest of it, like the ladies he had seen when he'd visited Ken in hospital, but on Marcia's dressing gown he did not like to speculate. In a curious way he found himself sheering away from her and turning his thoughts to something else. In any case a shout from his landlady – some complaint about the smell of frying – soon brought him back to earth again.

Most of Norman's holiday was spent in this idle and profitless way. The truth was that he didn't really know what to do with himself when he wasn't working. In the last week he had to visit the dentist, to adjust his new plate and to practise eating with it. The dentist was a Yorkshireman and rather too jolly for Norman's liking, and although he was National Health Norman had to fork out quite a lot of money for a considerable amount of discomfort. Thank you for nothing! he thought bitterly. When he was reasonably confident of being able to attempt something more than soup or macaroni cheese, Norman went back to work. He had a few days leave still in hand. 'You never know when they might come in useful,' he said, but he felt that those extra days would never be needed, but would accumulate like a pile of dead leaves drifting on to the pavement in autumn.

Six

Letty was not altogether surprised to get the letter from Marjorie saying that she was going to marry David Lydell. So much can change in such a short time especially, it would appear, if one is living in a village, though Letty didn't quite see why this should be so.

'David and I found that we were just two lonely people with so much to give each other,' Marjorie wrote.

Letty had not realized that her friend might have been lonely. Her life as a widow living in the country had always seemed so enviable, so full of trivial but absorbing doings.

'The vicarage is so uncomfortable,' the letter went on. 'There is a *great* deal to be done there. And would you believe it, the estate agent tells me that I can ask (and get!) £20,000 for the cottage! Of course you will realize that there is only one slight worry and that is you, dear old Letty. It will hardly be possible (and I don't for a moment suppose you would wish it) for you to come and live with us at the vicarage when you retire. So it's occurred to me that you might like to take a room at Holmhurst where I *think* there may well be a vacancy shortly (due to *death,* of course!), only you must let me know soon because . . .' Here the letter went into further tedious detail, the upshot of it being that Marjorie could 'get Letty in' because she knew the woman who ran it. It was not by any means an old people's home because of course only selected applicants would be accepted, on a *personal* recommendation . . .

Letty did not bother to read the last part of the letter very carefully. Marjorie went on with what seemed like girlish enthusiasm, but no doubt a woman in love, even if she is over sixty, feels no less rapturous than a girl of nineteen. Skimming over the final page, Letty learned that David was such a fine person; he had been so lonely and misunderstood in his last parish and some people in the village hadn't been too kind. Finally, they were so much in love that the difference in their ages ('I am of course some ten years older than he is') didn't make the slightest difference. Letty reflected that the difference must be nearer twenty years than ten but she was prepared to accept the fact of their love even if she could not understand it. Love was a mystery she had never experienced. As a young woman she had wanted to love, had felt that she ought to, but it had not come about. This lack in her was something she had grown used to and no longer thought about, but it was disconcerting, even a little shocking, to find that Marjorie was by no means beyond it.

Of course there was no question of her living at Holmhurst, a large red-brick mansion standing in wide lawns which she had often passed when she went to see Marjorie. She had once noticed an old woman with a lost expression peering through one of the surrounding hedges and that impression had remained with her. When her retirement day came, and it was not far off now, she would no doubt stay in her bed-sitting room for the time being. One could lead a very pleasant life in London – museums and art galleries, concerts and theatres – all those things that cultured people in the country were said to miss and crave for would be at Letty's disposal. Of course she would have to answer Marjorie's letter, to offer her congratulations (for surely that was the word) and to ease her conscience about the upsetting of the retirement plans, but not necessarily by return of post.

On her way home Letty noticed a barrow selling flowers near the Underground station. It occurred to her that she might buy a bunch for her landlady who had invited all the tenants to coffee that evening – not all-the-year-round chrysanthemums, but something small and unobtrusive like anemones or violets; but nothing of that sort was available and one could not buy the daisy-like flowers, dyed turquoise blue or red-ink pink, which were being offered as a bargain, so Letty walked on without buying anything. As she approached the house she was overtaken by Marya, the Hungarian who also lived there, carrying a bunch of the turquoise-dyed flowers that Letty had rejected.

'So pretty,' she said enthusiastically, 'and only 10p. You remember, Miss Embrey has asked us to coffee, so I thought, one takes flowers.'

Letty now realized that Marya had got the better of her, as she often did, filling the bathroom with her dripping clothes and taking Letty's *Daily Telegraph* in pretended mistake for her own lesser paper.

Miss Embrey lived on the ground floor and her three tenants – Letty, Marya and Miss Alice Spurgeon – came out of their rooms like animals emerging from burrows and descended the stairs at half past eight.

How aggressively nice and good her 'things' were, Letty thought, as she accepted a cup of coffee in Miss Embrey's Crown Derby. And now, it appeared, she was taking herself and these nice things to a home for gentlewomen in the country, perhaps the very home that Letty had decided to reject.

'My brother has arranged it all for me.' Miss Embrey smiled as she gave them this information, perhaps because she realized that none of her tenants had a man to arrange things for her. They were all unmarried women and no man had ever been known to visit them, not even a relative.

'Arthur has dealt with *everything*,' Miss Embrey stressed, and this included the house which was to be – indeed had already been – sold, with the tenants in it, quite a usual practice.

'And who is to be our new landlord?' Miss Spurgeon was the first to put their thoughts into words.

'A very nice gentleman,' said Miss Embrey in her mildest manner. 'He and his family will occupy the ground floor and basement.'

'It is a large family?' Marya asked.

'I understand a near relative may be sharing the accommodation with him. It is good to know that the ties of blood and kinship are still respected in some parts of the world.'

This led Letty to ask tentatively whether their new landlord was perhaps not English – a foreigner, if one could put it like that, and Miss Embrey was equally circumspect in her answer, implying that, in a manner of speaking, he was.

'What is his name?' Marya asked.

'Mr Jacob Olatunde.' Miss Embrey pronounced the syllables carefully, as if she had been practising them.

'He is black, then?' Again it was Marya, the Hungarian, who dared to ask the blunt question.

'Certainly his skin is not what is usually regarded as white, but which of us, for example, could say that we were white?' Miss Embrey looked round at her three tenants – Letty, with a pinkish skin, Marya, a sallow olive, Miss Spurgeon, parchment – all quite different. 'As you know, I have lived in China, so these distinctions of skin colour mean very little to me. Mr Olatunde comes from Nigeria,' she declared.

Miss Embrey sat back and folded her hands one over the other, those pale, useless hands exceptionally spotted with brown, and offered more coffee.

Only Marya, toadyish with her murmurs of 'such delicious coffee', accepted the offer. Miss Embrey smiled and poured her another cup. It was not the expensive blend of freshly ground beans that she would have offered to guests of her own choosing. Nor were the peculiar dyed flowers that Marya had pressed upon her the sort of decoration she would choose for her drawing room, so in a sense it was tit for tat.

'That is clear, then?' she declared, the chairman closing the meeting. 'Mr Olatunde will be your landlord from the Michaelmas quarter day.'

Afterwards there was talk on the stairs as the tenants went back to their rooms.

'We must remember that until very recently Nigeria was British,' said Miss Spurgeon. 'It was pink on the map. In some old atlases it still is.'

Letty felt that with the way things were going nothing was pink on the map any more. That night, as she lay in bed finding it difficult to sleep, the whole of her life seemed to unroll before her like that of a drowning man ... is said to do, she thought, for of course her experience did not extend to drowning and it was unlikely that it ever would. Death, when it came, would present itself in another guise, something more 'suitable' for a person like herself, for where would she ever be likely to be in danger of death by drowning?

'It never rains but it pours,' said Norman the next morning when Letty had told them in the office about the new development in her retirement plans. 'First your friend getting married and now this – whatever next? There'll be a third thing, just you wait.'

'Yes, troubles do tend to come in threes, or so people say,' Edwin remarked. There was of course an undeniable interest and even unadmitted pleasure in the contemplation of other people's misfortunes, and for a moment Edwin basked in this, shaking his head and speculating on what the third disaster might be.

'Don't tell us you're getting married too,' said Norman jauntily. 'That might be the third thing.'

Letty had to smile, as she was meant to, at such a fantastic suggestion. 'No chance of that,' she said. 'But I can still go and live in the country if I want to. There's a nice house in the village where I could get a room.'

'An old people's home?' Norman asked, quick as a flash.

'Not exactly – you can have your own furniture there.'

'An old people's home where you can have your own furniture – your bits and pieces and treasures,' Norman went on.

'Of course you won't necessarily have to leave your room in London,' said Edwin. 'The new landlord may be a very good man. A lot of splendid West Africans come to our church and they do very well in the sanctuary. They have a great love of ritual and pageantry.'

This was cold comfort to Letty, for it was these very qualities that she feared, the noise and exuberance, all those characteristics exemplified by the black girl in the office which were so different from her own.

'Oh, she'll find their way of life so different,' said Norman, 'the cooking smell and that. I know about bedsitters, believe me.'

Marcia had so far contributed nothing to the discussion for there was a fear in her mind, even if it was not a very strong one, that she might have to offer Letty a room in her house. After all, Letty had always been kind to her; she had once offered to make her a cup of tea before going home, and even though the offer had not been accepted it had not been forgotten. But this did not mean that Marcia was under any obligation to provide accommodation for Letty in her retirement. For of course it would be impossible – she couldn't have anybody else living in her house. Two women could never share the same kitchen, she told herself, forgetting for the moment that she never really used the kitchen except to boil a kettle or make a piece of toast. Then there would be the difficulty of the store cupboard where Marcia kept her collection of tinned foods, and the special and rather unusual arrangement she had about milk bottles, not to mention the use of the bathroom and the arrangement of personal washing – the difficulties were insuperable. Women alone had to make their own way in the world and no doubt Letty already knew this. And if she couldn't cope there would be somebody like Janice Brabner coming round, asking personal questions, making stupid suggestions and inviting her to do things she didn't want to do. It certainly wasn't Marcia's duty to offer a home to Letty, just because she had a house of her own and lived by herself. Indignation welled up inside her, and she asked herself, why should I? But there was no answer to this question because nobody asked it. Nobody had even thought of it, let alone Letty herself.

'I'll wait and see what happens,' she said sensibly. 'After all, one doesn't want to go looking for new accommodation in August. It's not a very good time.'

'August is a wicked month,' said Norman, who had seen the phrase somewhere.

Not wicked so much as awkward, Edwin thought. August 15th – Feast of the Assumption, Solemn Mass 8 p.m. There might not be the full complement of servers, even with the splendid West Africans, and people were disinclined to attend an evening Mass at the end of a hot summer day. You'd have thought Rome would have chosen a more convenient time. But the Doctrine of the Assumption had been proclaimed about 1950, he believed, and church life in the Italy of twenty years ago was no doubt rather different from present-day practice in England in the seventies, even in a High Anglican church, where most of the population didn't go to church anyway and those that did might well be away on holiday. Some people thought Father G. went rather too far –

'way out' – in observing some of these so-called obligations, but of course Edwin would be there this evening, among the two or three gathered together, and that was the main thing.

'I may get on very well with Mr Olatunde,' Letty was saying, in a bright, brave tone. 'I certainly shan't do anything in a hurry.'

Seven

JANICE ALWAYS HAD to nerve herself before going to see Marcia again. She wasn't like the other old ladies she visited, in fact the term 'old lady' didn't seem to describe her, yet she wasn't eccentric in a quaint or lovable way either. But there were always people like this – one had to regard it as a challenge, to try to get through to Marcia, to understand what went on in her mind.

Janice decided to choose Saturday morning rather than an evening for her next visit. People who worked were usually in on Saturday morning and with some, though not with Marcia, there might be the chance of a cup of coffee if one chose a suitable time. Still, she did open the door and that was something.

'How have things been with you?' Janice asked, stepping into the hall uninvited, but one must 'gain access', that was very important. 'Have you been managing your housework all right?' The dust on the hall table told its own story and the floor looked grey and gritty. Real nitty-gritty, Janice smiled at the fancy. But of course one mustn't smile – how *had* she been coping? She wished Marcia would make some remark, however trite, instead of staring at her in that unnerving way. There was a shopping basket on a chair in the hall. This could be a talking point and Janice seized on it with relief.

'I see you've been shopping.'

'Yes. Saturday is my shopping day.'

This at least was encouraging, that she had a shopping day, just like any other woman. But what had she bought? Nothing but tinned food, it seemed. A word of tactful criticism and friendly advice was needed here. Fresh vegetables, even if only a cabbage, would be better than processed peas, and apples or oranges than tinned peaches. She ought to be able to afford suitable food, but perhaps she didn't want to eat sensibly, that was the annoying and irritating thing about the people one went to see. But of course she had been in hospital; she was still 'under the doctor', as the expression was. Didn't he ever enquire into her diet?

'I always like to have plenty of tinned foods in the house,' Marcia said in a rather grand manner when Janice tried to suggest that fresh food would be better for her.

'Oh, yes, of course. Tins are very useful, especially when you can't get out or don't want to go to the shops.' No point in going on to somebody like Marcia who obviously wouldn't be led or advised by anyone. Janice was getting to know that she was the kind of person one mustn't interfere with but just keep an eye on. It would be better not to make any comment on the housework or lack of it. Some people didn't like doing housework, anyway.

'Goodbye, then,' she said. 'I'll pop in again some time.'

When she had gone Marcia took her shopping bag to unpack it in the kitchen. Every week she bought some tins for her store cupboard and now she spent some time arranging them. There was a good deal of classifying and sorting to be done here; the tins could be arranged according to size or by types of food – meat, fish, fruit, vegetables, soup or miscellaneous. This last category included such unclassifiable items as tomato puree, stuffed vine leaves (this was an impulse buy) and tapioca pudding. There was work to be done here and Marcia enjoyed doing it.

Then, as the day was fine, she went into the garden and picked her way over the long uncut grass to the shed where she kept milk bottles. These needed to be checked from time to time and occasionally she even went as far as dusting them. Sometimes she would put out one for the milkman but she mustn't let the hoard get too low because if there was a national emergency of the kind that seemed so frequent nowadays or even another war, there could well be a shortage of milk bottles and we might find ourselves back in the situation of 'No bottle, no milk', as in the last war. As she moved among the bottles Marcia was irritated to discover one of an alien brand among the United Dairy bottles – 'County Dairies', it said. Wherever had that come from? She didn't remember noticing it before and of course the milkman wouldn't take it back – they only collected their own bottles. She stood with it in her hand, frowning at the effort of trying to remember where it could possibly have come from. Then it dawned on her. Letty had given her some milk one day at the office. She had been staying with that friend of hers in the country and had brought back a pint of milk, had drunk some of it for her lunch, then given the rest to Marcia. So that was it. Marcia felt suddenly annoyed with Letty for having foisted this alien bottle on her. She must be made to take it back.

Seeing her coming out of the shed with a milk bottle in her hand, Nigel, the young man next door, told himself that here was a chance to show neighbourly friendliness, as his wife Priscilla was always urging him to.

'Would you like me to cut your grass, Miss Ivory?' he asked, going to the fence. 'I've got the mower out.' Though really, seeing its length, a scythe would be more appropriate.

'No, thank you,' said Marcia politely, 'I prefer the grass as it is,' and went into the house. She was still feeling annoyed with Letty about the milk bottle. There was certainly no question of her offering Letty a room in her house now; that was not at all the sort of person one wanted under the same roof.

That evening Letty crouched in her room, listening. It wasn't even a rowdy party, these bursts of hymn-singing and joyful shouts, for Mr Olatunde, her new landlord, was a priest of a religious sect. 'Aladura,' Miss Embrey had murmured, but the name meant nothing, only the coming and going in the house and the noise. Now perhaps Letty really did feel like a drowning man, with the events of her past life unrolling before her, those particular events which had led her to this. How had it come about that she, an Englishwoman born in Malvern in 1914 of middle-class English parents, should find herself in this room in London surrounded by enthusiastic, shouting, hymn-singing Nigerians? It must surely be because she had not married. No man had taken her away and immured her in some comfortable suburb where hymn-singing was confined to Sundays and nobody was fired with enthusiasm. Why had this not happened? Because she had thought that love was a necessary ingredient for marriage? Now, having looked around her for forty years, she was not so sure. All those years wasted, looking for love! The thought of it was enough to bring about silence in the house and during the lull she plucked up the courage to go downstairs and tap – too timidly, she felt – at Mr Olatunde's door.

'I wonder if you could make a little less noise?' she asked. 'Some of us find it rather disturbing.'

'Christianity *is* disturbing,' said Mr Olatunde.

It was difficult to know how to answer this. Indeed Letty found it impossible so Mr Olatunde continued, smiling, 'You are a Christian lady?'

Letty hesitated. Her first instinct had been to say 'yes', for of course one was a Christian lady, even if one would not have put it quite like that. How was she to explain to this vital, ebullient black man her own blend of Christianity – a grey, formal, respectable thing of measured observances and mild general undemanding kindness to all? 'I'm sorry,' she said, drawing back, 'I didn't mean . . .' What had she meant? Confronted by these smiling people she felt she could hardly repeat her complaint about the noise.

A handsome woman in a long brightly coloured dress and head tie stepped forward. 'We are having supper now,' she said. 'You will join us?'

Letty was reminded of Norman as a rich spicy smell was wafted towards her. She thanked the woman politely, saying that she had already eaten.

'I'm afraid you would not like our Nigerian cooking,' said Mr Olatunde, with a touch of complacency.

'No, perhaps not.' Letty withdrew, embarrassed by the crowd of smiling faces that seemed to be pressing in on her. We are not the same, she thought hopelessly. She wondered what Edwin and Norman and Marcia would have done in the circumstances, but came to no conclusions. Other people's reactions were unpredictable and while she could imagine Edwin entering into the religious aspect of the evening and even taking part in the service, it might well be that Norman and Marcia, usually so set in their isolation, would in some surprising way have been drawn into the friendly group. Only Letty remained outside.

Eight

THERE HAD ALREADY been a good deal of talk in the office about Letty's situation and what she ought to do about it, and as time went on the question became more urgent, especially when Marya found a living-in job as housekeeper to a family in Hampstead, and Miss Spurgeon made arrangements to go into an old people's home.

'You'll be alone in the house now,' said Norman gleefully. 'It'll seem strange, won't it?' Perhaps this was the third misfortune he had prophesied, proving that disasters always went in threes.

'Your new landlord is a clergyman, isn't he?' said Marcia.

'Yes, in a manner of speaking.' Letty had a vision of Father Lydell leaning back in Marjorie's armchair, eyes closed, sipping Orvieto, so very different from Mr Olatunde. Obviously there were clergymen and clergymen, she thought. 'I wouldn't want to hurt his feelings,' she said, 'by anything I said about the people living in the house. He seems to be a very nice man.'

'Isn't there some friend you could live with?' Edwin suggested. 'Apart from the one who's getting married?' A woman like Letty must have many friends, a whole army of nice women like the WRVS or some – though not all – of the female congregation of his church. Surely there were plenty of such women? One saw them everywhere.

'The best thing is to have a relative,' said Norman. 'Then they're bound to do something for you. After all, blood is thicker than water, however distant the connection – you can bank on that.'

Letty considered some of her cousins, not seen since childhood, now living somewhere in the west of England. She could hardly expect any of them to offer her a home.

'Have you ever thought of taking a lodger?' Edwin asked, turning to Marcia.

'The money might be useful,' Norman chipped in, 'when you're retired.'

'Oh, I shan't need money,' said Marcia impatiently. 'There won't be any need for me to take in lodgers.' 'Unthinkable' was the word that came to her at Edwin's suggestion, the idea of offering a home to Letty, especially when she remembered that milk bottle. But Letty wouldn't like it either. Even now she was protesting, obviously embarrassed for Marcia as well as for herself.

'There are organizations and people wanting to help ladies,' said Edwin quaintly.

'There's a young woman who comes round to see me sometimes – seems to think I need help.' Marcia laughed in a mirthless way. 'It's the other way round, if you ask me.'

'But you have been in hospital,' Edwin reminded her. 'I expect that's why they like to keep an eye on you.'

'Oh, yes, but I go to Mr Strong's clinic for that.' Marcia smiled. 'I don't need young people telling me not to buy tinned peas.'

'Well, it's good to know that people do care,' said Letty vaguely, feeling that it might go rather beyond tinned peas. 'I expect something will turn up when I retire – after all, I haven't retired yet.'

'But you soon will,' said Norman, 'and you won't get much of a pension from here to add to what the state gives you. And then there's inflation to be considered,' he added unhelpfully.

'Inflation isn't exactly the kind of thing you can consider,' said Letty. 'It just comes on you unawares.'

'You're telling me,' said Norman, and delving in his pocket he produced the checkout payslip from his latest visit to the supermarket. 'Just listen to this,' and he proceeded to read it out. It was the increase in the prices of tinned soup and butter beans that seemed to anger him most, giving a strange insight into his daily diet.

Nobody commented or even listened. Marcia thought complacently of her well-stocked store cupboard and Letty decided she would have an early lunch and then take a bus to the Oxford Street shops. Only Edwin, perhaps seeing himself as a person wanting to help ladies, went on thinking about Letty and her problem.

All Saints' Day, the first of November, fell on a weekday. There was an evening Mass, quite well attended, and on the next Sunday Edwin was present at the ceremony of coffee and biscuits after the morning service of Parish Communion at a church he sometimes went to because he had once lived in the neighbourhood. It was not his regular church but he had chosen it especially with Letty in mind.

The making of coffee was in itself a ritual entrusted to various women members of the congregation, all of whom knew Edwin from his occasional visits to the church, and as he entered the hall, a bleak room garishly decorated by members of the youth club, he heard the voice of an old woman raised in a protest about biscuits.

'It is quite unnecessary to have biscuits with the coffee,' she said. 'A hot drink is all that anyone needs.'

'I like to have something to nibble with my coffee,' protested a little furry woman in a grey coat. 'We all know that Mrs Pope is wonderful for her age but the elderly don't *need* much to eat. If it had been known beforehand that the biscuit tin was empty something could have been done about it – it could have been replenished – biscuits could have been bought.'

Into the middle of this controversy Edwin inserted himself with what seemed like a brutal attack. 'I believe one of you ladies has a spare room,' he declared.

There was silence, an awkward silence, Edwin felt, and both the women began to make excuses like the guests bidden to the marriage feast – the room was hardly more than a cupboard, it had all the things for the church bazaar in it, it might be needed for a relative. This last was the trump card but Edwin persevered. He had not thought out what he would do next, and he now realized that it might have been better if he had begun by describing Letty and outlining the nature of her problem, emphasizing her need for a room, so that consciences might be played upon and hearts touched. But how should he describe Letty? As a friend? She was hardly that and being a single woman might arouse gossip. A lady I know? That sounded too arch and coy. A woman who works in my office? Surely that would be best. The words woman, work, office, presented a reassuring picture of somebody of the preferred sex, who would be out all day and might even be a congenial companion on the occasions when she was in the house.

So Edwin went on, adopting a confidential tone, 'You see, it's like this. A woman who works in my office is in a difficulty. The house where she lives has been sold with the tenants in it and the new landlord and his family aren't quite what she's been used to, rather noisy, in fact.'

'Blacks?' asked Mrs Pope sharply.

'That's about the size of it,' Edwin admitted in a genial way.

'Mind you, Mr Olatunde is a very good man – a priest, in a manner of speaking.'

'How can he be a priest in a manner of speaking?' asked Mrs Pope. 'He must be either a priest or not a priest. There can be no qualification.'

'He is a priest of an African religious sect,' Edwin explained. 'And of course the services are not quite like ours – there's a lot of noisy singing and shouting.'

'And this woman – lady – she is that, I assume?'

'Oh, certainly. There would be no difficulty on that score,' said Edwin casually, feeling that Letty was in every way superior, if that was the criterion to be applied.

'She finds the noise too much where she is living?'

'Yes, she does, being a very quiet person herself.' That was something to be emphasized.

'Of course there *is* my large back room, and it might be useful to have another person in the house.'

Edwin recalled that Mrs Pope lived alone.

'If one fell downstairs or tripped over a rug and was unable to get up . . .'

'You might lie for hours before anyone came,' said the little furry woman eagerly.

'One's bones are so brittle,' said Mrs Pope. 'A fracture could lead to serious complications.'

Edwin felt that they were getting off the point. He wanted the business to be settled, with Letty in the room. Of course Mrs Pope was old, but she was active and independent and he was sure that Letty, being a woman, would be very helpful in case of illness or accident. Now he could see the whole pattern emerging, with Letty's life governed by the soothing rhythm of the Church's year. All Saints' today, then All Souls'; everybody could share in the commemoration of the saints and the departed. Then would come Advent followed closely – too closely, it often seemed – by

Christmas. After Christmas came Boxing Day, the Feast of St Stephen, hardly observed as such unless it happened to be one's patronal festival; then the Innocents, St John the Evangelist and Epiphany. The Conversion of St Paul and Candlemas (where one usually sang one of Keble's less felicitous hymns) were followed all too soon by the Sundays before Lent, but the evenings were drawing out. Ash Wednesday was an important landmark – evening Mass and the Imposition of Ashes, the black smudge on the forehead, 'dust thou art and to dust shalt thou return' – some people didn't like that, thought it 'morbid' or 'not very nice'.

'There *is* a basin with hot and cold water in the room and she could use the bathroom occasionally. She wouldn't need a bath every night, would she?' Too much washing was bad for the skin, the constant immersion in hot water dried out the natural oils ... Mrs Pope was coming round to the idea of Letty while Edwin was taking her through the Church's year, but he would hardly be able to answer questions about how often she would want a bath.

Everybody knew about Lent, of course, even if they didn't do anything about it, with Palm Sunday ushering in the services of Holy Week – not what they used to be, certainly, but there was still something left of Maundy Thursday, Good Friday and Holy Saturday with the ceremonies, the prelude to Easter Day. Low Sunday always seemed a bit of an anticlimax after all that had gone before but it wasn't long before Ascension Day and then Whit Sunday or Pentecost as it was properly called. After that you had Corpus Christi, with a procession out of doors if fine, and then Trinity Sunday, followed by all those long hot summer Sundays, with the green vestments and the occasional saint's day ... That was how it had always been and how it would go on in spite of trendy clergy trying to introduce so-called up-to-date forms of worship, rock and roll and guitars and discussions about the Third World instead of Evensong. The only difficulty was that Edwin wasn't at all sure that Letty ever went to church. She had never mentioned it when he talked about such things in the office. Still, when she was settled in Mrs Pope's back room and when she had retired, there was no knowing how her life would change.

Nine

'So you are Miss Crowe.'

It was not the most friendly greeting, Letty felt, but there was nothing for it but to repeat that she was indeed Miss Crowe and to assume that the woman peering through the barely opened door must be Mrs Pope. And why should she have expected friendliness when the relationship between them was to be that of landlady and tenant? Friendliness was by no means to be taken for granted. Obviously she should have expected little in the way of warmth, with the taxi taking her what seemed so very far north, though the postal address was only NW6.

It was not long before Christmas – St Lucy's Day, Edwin had reminded her, though the saint seemed to have no particular significance for the move. Norman, of course, made much of it being the shortest day. 'Get there in good time,' he advised. 'You don't want to be wandering about in a strange district after dark.'

'One has to be careful,' Mrs Pope went on, opening the door a little wider. 'There are so many impostors these days.'

Letty had to agree, though she felt that Mrs Pope was not the sort of person to be taken in by an impostor. While Edwin's impression and description of her had been merely that of a woman in her eightieth year who was 'wonderful for her age', Letty now saw that she was an imposing figure with noble almost Roman features and a mass of thick white hair, of the kind that is sometimes described as 'abundant', arranged in an elaborate old-fashioned style.

After the vitality and warmth of Mr Olatunde's house Mrs Pope's seemed bleak and silent, with its heavy dark furniture and ticking grandfather clock, the kind of tick that would keep one awake until one got used to it. Letty was shown the kitchen where she could prepare her meals and a cupboard where she could keep her food. The bathroom and lavatory were indicated with gestures, being not the kind of rooms into which one would show people. The lavatory window, Letty saw when she went in, looked out on to back gardens, with blackened stumps on the frosty earth, and beyond them the railway, where trains rattled by in a kind of hinterland which marked their first emergence from the Underground. Not really the kind of district where one would choose to live, but of course it was only temporary and 'beggars can't be choosers', as Norman lost no time in reminding her.

The room itself was quite pleasant, sparsely furnished, which was a good thing, and there was a basin with hot and cold water, as Edwin had said. Letty felt like a governess in a Victorian novel arriving at a new post, but there would be no children here and no prospect of a romantic attachment to the widower master of the house or a handsome son of the family. Her own particular situation had hardly existed in the past, for now it was the unattached working woman, the single 'business lady' of the advertisements, who was most likely to arrive in the house of strangers. Letty had often found herself doing this, arranging her clothes in the drawers and wardrobe provided and putting out her personal possessions, the things that might give some clue as to what sort of person she was. There were her books – anthologies of poetry, though nothing later than *Poems of Today. Second Series* – her current library book; her transistor radio, a bowl of hyacinths nearly in flower, her knitting in a flowered cretonne bag. There were no photographs, not even of her friend Marjorie or of her old home, her parents, a cat or a dog.

At least Mrs Pope was leaving her to herself this first evening, Letty thought, as she prepared a poached egg on toast in the silent kitchen. Later, as she lay in bed, unable to sleep on her first night in a strange bed that would soon become as familiar as her own body, she realized that she had taken action, she had made the move, she had coped. In the sleepless hours she heard footsteps on the landing and a sudden thump. Supposing Mrs Pope had a fall? She was an elderly person and heavy – lifting her would be difficult. Letty hoped she wasn't going to have to do that kind of coping, but eventually she fell asleep and heard nothing more.

Next morning in the office there was an air of expectancy, almost of excitement. They all wanted to know how Letty had got on in her new room. Edwin had a proprietary attitude towards the move – after all, he was entitled to it as he had found the room for her, and the others felt that he had done something pretty good in, as it were, delivering her from Mr Olatunde. 'I only hope it won't be a case of frying pan into fire,' Norman observed. 'You must watch out that you don't get landed with an elderly person and all *that* entails.'

'Oh, Mrs Pope is very independent,' Edwin said quickly. 'She's a member of the parochial church council and a very active one.'

'That's as may be,' said Norman, 'but it doesn't necessarily follow that she's got perfect control over her legs – she might fall, you know.'

'Yes, that thought came to me in the night,' said Letty, 'but it might happen to anyone. We could all fall.'

Nobody seemed inclined to go into the deeper implications of what Letty had just said, but Edwin repeated now what he had thought when he first broached the subject to Mrs Pope. 'Oh, a woman can deal with these things easily enough,' he reminded Norman in a rather sharp tone. 'There's no need to make the kind of fuss you or I would make if we were faced with such a situation.'

'Equal opportunities!' said Norman. 'That's one of the things we men prefer to leave to the ladies. Anyway, what is one's responsibility in that kind of thing – answer me that?'

'Just the ordinary responsibility of one human being towards another,' said Letty. 'I hope I should do whatever was best.'

'But sometimes it's unwise to move a person who has fallen,' Norman persisted. 'You could do more harm than good.'

'You should ring for the ambulance,' said Marcia, making her first contribution to the discussion. 'The ambulance men know what to do. Are you able to use the kitchen when you want to?' she went on, still feeling the very smallest tinge of guilt at not having offered to take in Letty herself, but of course, as she repeatedly told herself, it would *not* have done. And once again she had forgotten to bring that milk bottle to the office.

'Yes, that seems to work all right. I cooked supper and breakfast – there's an electric cooker and I'm used to that, and plenty of room for me to keep my own things.'

'It's so important to have plenty of room for tins,' said Marcia. 'You should insist on that. You wouldn't want to keep everything in the room where you sleep.'

'I have to keep everything in the one room,' said Norman.

'Well, beggars can't be choosers, as you're so fond of reminding us,' said Edwin. 'I only hope this move will turn out to be a good thing,' he added. 'I shall feel responsible for it if anything goes wrong.'

'You mustn't feel that,' Letty reassured him. 'It's up to oneself, to adapt to circumstances.'

'Up to you to make a go of it,' said Norman chirpily. 'That's the ticket.'

Mrs Pope waited until Letty had left the house before she went upstairs from her ground-floor sitting room. She will walk down to the bus stop or take the Underground, she thought, as she entered Letty's room, knowing that she would not be back before half past six.

Letty had not asked for a key to the room and Mrs Pope felt that she had a duty to see that everything was in order. It would also be just as well to judge from her possessions what kind of a person her new lodger was.

The first thing that struck Mrs Pope was tidiness and order. This was a slight disappointment for she had hoped to find interesting things lying about in the room. Naturally she would expect somebody recommended by Mr Braithwaite – she did not think of him as 'Edwin' – to be respectable, even a churchwoman, but she was surprised to find that there was no devotional book on the bedside table, not even a Bible, just a novel from the Camden library. Mrs Pope would have respected a biography but she was not interested in novels and did not give the book a second glance. Turning her attention to the washbasin she noted talcum powder and deodorant, a jar of skinfood and a tube of Steradent tablets besides toothbrushes and paste and a new flower-patterned face flannel. The little cupboard over the basin held only aspirins and vegetable laxative tablets, no exotic drugs of any kind, though she might well carry tablets in her handbag. The dressing table had a selection of cosmetics on it, all neatly ranged. Glancing over her shoulder towards the door, Mrs Pope opened the top drawer. It contained several neatly folded pairs of stockings or tights, gloves, scarves and a small leather jewel box. In the jewel box were a small string of pearls, obviously not real, two or three strings of beads, a few pairs of earrings and two rings, one gold with a half-hoop of small diamonds (her mother's engagement ring?), and the other a cheap butterfly-wing in a silver setting. Nothing of value or interest there, Mrs Pope decided. The chest of drawers held underwear, immaculately clean and folded, and jumpers and blouses, equally neat and clean. The contents of the wardrobe were more or less what might have been expected from the rest of the room and Mrs Pope did no more than glance at the hanging dresses, suits and skirts. There was a trouser suit, too, the kind of thing women of Letty's age had taken to wearing, and that too was as respectable and appropriate as the rest of the garments. Only one item caught Mrs Pope's eye, a rather gaily patterned cotton kimono, which seemed not to be in character with the rest of Miss Crowe's things. Had it perhaps been a gift from somebody in the mission field, a relative out there? There were some things one could hardly ask but no doubt she would see Miss Crowe coming out of the bathroom wearing it one day. Dissatisfied, Mrs Pope went downstairs again. The most one could say, and it seemed hardly enough, was that Miss Crowe seemed to be the ideal lodger or at least nothing could be gleaned to the contrary.

Ten

'Christmas comes but once a year,
And when it comes it brings good cheer . . .'

NORMAN RECITED THE tag with a touch of sarcasm in his voice. Nobody disputed the fact or took exception to his tone, for Christmas is a difficult time for those who are no longer young and are without close relatives or dependents, and each one in the office was thinking of the particular trials and difficulties the so-called festive season would bring with it. Only Edwin would be spending Christmas in the traditional and accepted way in his role as father and grandfather. 'Christmas is a time for the children,' people were apt to say, and he was prepared to accept this and go along with it, though he would much have preferred to spend the festival alone at home, with no more than a quick drink with Father G. between services to mark the secular aspect of the occasion.

Norman himself had been invited to eat his Christmas dinner with his brother-in-law Ken and his lady friend, the woman who was presumably to replace his dead wife, Norman's sister. 'After all, he has nobody,' they said, as they had when they allowed Norman to visit Ken in hospital. 'Might as well help them get through their turkey,' was the way Norman regarded the invitation, and as there was no public transport on that day Ken would call for him and bring him back by car so there would be no difficulty there. The hated motor car did occasionally have its uses.

It was the women – Letty and Marcia – who were the real worry, or 'posed something of a problem', as Janice Brabner put it. They had no relatives they could spend Christmas with and the season had for many years now been an occasion to be got through as quickly as possible. Letty had often spent the holiday with her friend in the country but this year Marjorie had Father Lydell, for ever fixed in Letty's memory as leaning back in a comfortable chair sipping an appropriate wine, no doubt a burgundy or even a mulled claret to suit the season, but whatever it was she felt she would be an intruder this year and in any case no invitation had been forthcoming. In this lack Letty was conscious of Marjorie's embarrassment at having to withhold it, so the season would not be one of unmixed happiness and relaxation for Marjorie either. In war there are no victors, as the saying went, and inappropriate though the idea might be there was still something applicable in it.

Marcia worried less about Christmas as the years went on. When her mother had been alive it had been a quiet time, marked only by the cooking of a larger than usual bird – their butcher usually recommended 'a nice capon' as being suitable for two ladies spending Christmas alone – and the provision of special food as well as titbits from the bird for Snowy, the old cat. After her mother's death Snowy had been enough company for Marcia, and when he had gone there was no special point about Christmas Day and it tended to merge into the rest of the holiday until it was no different from any other part of it.

'We must do something about Miss Ivory.' Nigel and Priscilla were agreed on that. Christmas was the time for 'doing' something about old people or 'the aged', as the nobler phrase described them, though that, in Priscilla's mind, conjured up pictures of tiny frail oriental ladies rather than people like Miss Ivory.

'It's the loneliness that's the worst part – or so one hears,' Priscilla said. 'The poor souls just long for somebody to talk to.' One evening she had met Janice Brabner trying to call on Marcia but getting no answer to her ringing and knocking. 'No joy whatsoever,' as she put it, though 'joy' was hardly the word. Janice was going away for Christmas and was worried about Marcia, so Priscilla had promised to keep an eye on her, even to ask her in for a meal, and what more suitable occasion than the turkey on Christmas Day?

Nigel had been a bit doubtful about this. 'She isn't all that old,' he had objected. 'She's independent enough to go out to work even though she's so odd. I suppose it would be kind to ask her but I can't quite see her fitting in with your grandparents.'

'Perhaps she'll refuse the invitation,' said Priscilla, 'but I feel I must ask her.'

'She didn't want me to cut her lawn that time when I offered,' said Nigel hopefully.

'But Christmas is a bit different,' Priscilla said, and evidently this was what Marcia felt too for she even managed to smile when she was asked.

Of course the grandparents were terribly nice to her, so thankful were they not to be the kind of old people who needed to have something 'done' about them. Priscilla's grandmother was so elegantly pink and white, with her beautifully coiffed hair and neat, pastel-coloured clothes, such a contrast to Marcia, with that crudely dyed hair and a peculiarly awful dress in a most unbecoming shade of bright blue. The grandparents led such useful and busy lives in their retirement in Buckinghamshire – every day for them was so full and interesting and their stay with Priscilla in London would be filled with worthwhile activities, visits to theatres and art galleries. What did Marcia *do*, or rather what would she do when she retired next year? One hardly liked to speculate and the question, politely and kindly put, brought forth the sort of answer that got one nowhere. Nor did Marcia really do justice to the traditional Christmas fare. The discovery that she didn't drink had cast the first slight gloom on the proceedings and the hope that she would eat well was disappointed by the way she left most of her small helping on the side of her plate. She murmured something about being a very small eater but Priscilla thought she might at least have had the manners to make a show of eating when so much trouble had been taken. But then that was what Janice had warned her about – these people weren't necessarily rewarding, one just had to plod on. Perhaps it would have been easier if Marcia had been that much older, really *ancient*.

After lunch they sat round the fire for coffee and chocolates were handed round. Everyone felt comfortably sleepy and would have liked to flop down and close their eyes, but the presence of Marcia was inhibiting. It seemed impossible to drop off with that beady glance fixed on them. They were all relieved when she suddenly got up and said she must go.

'How will you spend the rest of the holiday?' Priscilla asked, as if she were determined to punish herself further. 'Have you something arranged for Boxing Day?'

'Boxing Day?' Marcia did not seem to understand what was meant by Boxing Day, but after a pause she declared rather grandly, 'We who work in offices do value our leisure time, so we don't need to make elaborate plans,' and of course everyone had to respect this, while thankful that they need not do anything more about her Christmas.

Next day Marcia rose late and spent the morning tidying out a drawer full of old newspapers and paper bags, something she had been meaning to do for a long time. Then she checked the contents of her store cupboard but did not eat anything until the evening when she opened a small tin of pilchards. It was one left over from

Snowy's store, so it was not really breaking into her reserves. She had heard or read somewhere that pilchards contained valuable protein, though this was not the reason why she had opened that particular tin. She did not even remember that the young doctor at the hospital had told her that she ought to eat more.

Letty had made up her mind to face Christmas with courage and a kind of deliberate boldness, a determination to hold the prospect of loneliness at bay. It wasn't really as if she minded being alone for she was used to it; it was rather the idea that people might find out that she had no invitation for the day and that they would pity her. She endured the newspaper articles and radio programmes pandering to the collective guilt-feeling of those who were neither old nor lonely nor fortunate enough to have an odd relative or neighbour they could invite into their homes at Christmas, telling herself that at least she needn't feel guilty at this festive season. Marjorie seemed to have none of these feelings either, Letty reflected, for she had made no mention of Letty joining her for Christmas, and had sent her card and present (bath foam and hand cream done up in a fancy package) particularly early, so that there could be no misunderstanding on that score. I wouldn't have wanted to go there anyway, Letty told herself stoutly, not with David Lydell there. Even with the heavy load of Christmas services he would no doubt find plenty of time to be with his fiancée and, remembering the picnic, Letty did not fancy herself in the role of gooseberry.

Letty therefore prepared to spend Christmas alone, for she understood that Mrs Pope would be going to stay with her sister who lived in a village in Berkshire. But at the last minute there was a change of plan, various telephone calls were made, and in the end Mrs Pope announced that she was not going away after all. The change of plan was the result of an argument about heating, Mrs Pope's sister apparently being too mean to switch on the storage heaters before January, and the cottage being not only cold but damp and poky as well.

'I shall *not* go, neither now or *ever*,' Mrs Pope declared, standing militant by the telephone in the full dignity of her eighty-odd years.

'Warmth is so important,' Letty said, remembering the office conversations about hypothermia.

'Have you anything special for your Christmas dinner?' Mrs Pope then asked.

It had not occurred to Letty that Mrs Pope might suggest any kind of festive sharing or pooling of resources, for they had not so far eaten together, though they had met in the kitchen preparing their individual breakfasts and suppers. She did not at first like to admit that she had bought a chicken, for it seemed almost brutish to contemplate eating even the smallest bird all by herself, but when she realized what was in Mrs Pope's mind she had to confess.

'I have some ham and a Christmas pudding, one I made last year, so it will be best if we have our meal together,' Mrs Pope said. 'It is ridiculous to think of two women in the same house eating separate Christmas dinners. Not that I really make any difference in what I eat at Christmas – it's most unwise for old people to gorge themselves at any time.'

So Letty had no alternative but to listen to Mrs Pope discoursing on her favourite topic of the excessive amount of food most people ate. It was not conducive to an enjoyable meal and Letty could not help feeling that on this occasion she might have done better if she had stayed in her room in Mr Olatunde's house. A jolly Nigerian Christmas would surely have included her, and not for the first time she began to wonder if she had done the right thing by moving. Still, Christmas Day had been lived through and was now nearly over, that was the main thing.

The radio offered a choice of comedy, with a braying studio audience, which she did not feel in the mood for, or carols, with their sad memories of childhood and the days that can never come back. So she took up her library book and sat reading, wondering what sort of a Christmas the others in the office had spent. Then she remembered that the Kensington sales started the day after Boxing Day and her spirits suddenly lifted.

'Pushing the boat out, aren't you?' said Norman, with unusual jollity, as Ken topped up his glass.

'Well, I always think a really good meal like the one we've just eaten deserves all the trimmings,' Ken said.

'I only hope you're not going to suffer for it.' Norman could hardly resist casting this small gloom on the festivities. After all, the last time he'd seen Ken he'd been lying prone in the men's surgical ward, feeling pretty sorry for himself. But now he seemed to have fallen on his feet all right with this girlfriend – Joyce her name was, shortened to Joy – who was not only quite good-looking and an excellent cook but had a bit of money of her own and had even passed the test of the Institute of Advanced Motorists, whatever that might mean. So Ken had good reason to push the boat out.

Still, let them get on with it, all lovey-dovey at the kitchen sink doing the washing-up, Norman thought, sitting by the fire, as they had insisted when he made a half-hearted offer of help.

'You put your feet up,' Joy said. 'Have a bit of a rest – after all, you're one of the world's workers.'

Norman supposed they all were, come to that, though he and Ken spent most of their working life sitting down anyway, Ken stuck in the passenger seat of a car on test and he, Norman, at his desk doing damn all. Still, he wasn't averse to a bit of a rest, especially after a good meal, and it was always nice to see a coal fire and not to have to worry about having the right coins for the meter.

'Where exactly does he live?' Joy was saying, her pink rubber-gloved hands plunged in the washing-up water.

'Norman? Oh, he's got a bedsitter – Kilburn Park way.'

'On his own all the time, is he? It must be a bit lonely.'

'Lots of people live on their own,' Ken pointed out.

'Still, at Christmas . . . it does seem sort of sad.'

'Well, we're having him here today, aren't we? I don't see what more we can do.'

'You've never thought of sharing?'

'*Sharing?* You have to be joking!'

'Oh, I don't mean *now*. But when your wife, when Marigold . . .' Joy brought out the name tentatively for she could never get used to it or believe that Ken's wife had really been christened so, 'when she passed on and you were left on your own . . .'

Ken waited in grim silence. Let her put into words what she was thinking, that he might have asked Norman – the brother-in-law with whom he hadn't a thing in common apart from having been married to his sister – to come and live in his house, was that it? Imagine sharing a house with Norman! The very idea of it was enough to give him the creeps, and thinking about how it might be made him smile, even want to laugh, so that the grim silence was relaxed and he playfully flicked a tea towel at his intended second wife.

Larking about in the kitchen, Norman thought, hearing the sound of laughter, but he wasn't really envious, his attitude being 'sooner him than me'. When Ken had deposited him on his doorstep from his brand new buttercup-yellow motor car, Norman returned to his bed-sitting room – quite well satisfied with his lot. This Christmas had certainly brought a bit of good cheer, but today's jollifications had been enough for him and he quite looked forward to getting back to the office and hearing how the others had got on.

*

In the train coming back from staying with his daughter and her family, Edwin felt drained and exhausted, but relieved. They'd wanted him to stay longer, of course, but he'd pleaded various pressing engagements, for after Christmas Day, with a somewhat inadequate 'Family Communion' as the main service (no High Mass), and Boxing Day with a surfeit of cold turkey and fractious children, he felt he'd had enough. His son-in-law dropped him at the station while the family went on to a pantomime where they were to be joined by the other grandparents and another lot of children. All a very jolly family party but not exactly his 'scene', as Norman might put it.

Taking out his diary, Edwin considered the days after Christmas. Today, December 27th, was St John the Evangelist and there should be a good High Mass this evening at St John's over the other side of the common – it was their patronal festival, of course, and the priest there was a friend of Father G.'s. Then there was the day after, December 28th, Holy Innocents – he'd try to get over to Hammersmith for that. People didn't seem to realize what a lot there was going on after Christmas, quite apart from the day itself.

Eleven

THE FIRST DAY they were back in the office was the second of January. None of them had really needed New Year's Day to recover from the celebrations of the night before because none of them had been to a party, but there had always been grumblings when in the past they had been obliged to work on the day. Now, of course, the extended holiday had seemed a little too long and they were all glad to be back to work.

'Or what passes for work,' as Norman remarked, tilting back in his chair and drumming his fingers on his empty table.

'It's always a bit slack at this time,' Letty said. 'One tries to get things done before Christmas.'

'To clear one's desk,' said Marcia importantly, using a phrase from long ago that had little or no reality in their present situation.

'And when you get back there's nothing on it,' said Norman peevishly. He was bored now that the first interest of hearing about other people's Christmases had evaporated.

'Well, this has come in,' said Edwin, holding up a cyclostyled notice. He passed it to Norman who read it out.

'A Memorial Service for a man who retired before we came,' he said. 'What's that got to do with us?'

'I didn't know he'd died,' said Letty. 'Wasn't he once chairman?'

'It was in *The Times*,' Edwin pointed out. 'One feels that perhaps this department ought to be represented.'

'They couldn't expect that if nobody knew him,' said Marcia.

'I suppose they'd send round a notice in case anybody wanted to go,' said Letty in her usual tolerant manner. 'After all, there might be some who'd worked with him.'

'But it's today,' said Norman indignantly. 'How could we go today, at such short notice? What's going to happen to the work?'

Nobody answered him.

'Twelve noon,' Norman read out scornfully. 'I like that! What do they think we are?'

'I think I shall go,' said Edwin, looking at his watch. 'I see it's at the church used by the university – rather a suitable setting for a Memorial Service for an agnostic.'

'I suppose you know the church, you've been there before?' Letty asked.

'Oh, yes, I know it all right,' said Edwin casually. 'Pretty undenominational, you might say. They have to cater for all sorts there, but I suppose there'll be somebody who knows what to do.'

'Let's hope so! Unless you feel like taking the service yourself,' said Norman sarcastically. He was irritated at Edwin taking what seemed to him like an unfair advantage, though where the advantage lay he could hardly have said.

The church was still decorated for Christmas, with stiff-looking poinsettias and sprigs of holly on the window ledges, but an expensive florist's arrangement of white chrysanthemums had been placed at the side of the altar, as if to emphasize the dual purpose of the church's present function.

Memorial services were not much in Edwin's line, particularly not when they commemorated persons with whom he had little or nothing in common. It wasn't as if they were like funerals, of which he had experienced his fair share – father, mother, wife and various in-law relatives. And it wasn't as if this was a proper Requiem Mass, more like a social gathering, with the smartly dressed women in hats and fur coats and the dark-suited men in good, heavy overcoats. They seemed very far removed from the little huddle of mourners Edwin associated with funerals he had attended. Of course the time of mourning had passed and this service was being held to celebrate the deceased's life and achievements, so there was a difference. Another noticeable difference was the warmth of the church on this January day. Reassuring wafts of hot air circulated round Edwin's feet and he noticed the woman in front of him loosening the collar of her fur coat.

The hymns chosen were 'He who would valiant be', and another with modern words that might seem to have been specially written so as not to offend the most militant agnostic or atheist, set to a tune that nobody seemed to know. There was a reading from Ecclesiastes and a short eulogy, delivered by a younger colleague of the deceased, quietly triumphant in the prime of life. Edwin had seen this person once or twice at the office, so he felt that his presence at the service was justified. After all, he was representing Norman, Letty and Marcia, and that was entirely fitting.

As he filed out with the congregation, Edwin noticed that some of them, instead of going out through the church door, seemed to be slipping into a half open side door into a kind of vestry. Not everyone was doing this, so it looked as if those who did were in some way favoured and Edwin soon saw why this was. Inside the vestry he glimpsed a table on which were ranged glasses of a drink that looked like sherry (it would hardly have been whisky, he felt). It was easy for Edwin to insinuate himself among the slippers-in and nobody questioned him; he looked very much the kind of person who had the right to be there, tall, grey and sombre.

Taking a glass of sherry – there was a choice of medium or dry, sweet evidently not having been considered appropriate to the occasion – Edwin looked around him, storing up impressions to tell them back in the office. His own observations took in the usual paraphernalia of the Anglican church that made this vestry much like any other of his experience – flower vases and candlesticks, an untidy pile of hymn books with the covers torn and no doubt pages missing inside, and a discarded crucifix of elaborate design, probably condemned by the brass ladies as impossible to clean. A crisp-looking terylene surplice was suspended from a hook on a cleaner's wire hanger and there were red cassocks and a few dusty old black ones hanging on a rail. But these details would probably not interest Norman, Letty and Marcia. They would want to know who was at the service and how they were behaving, what they were saying and doing.

'Well, at least we've given him some kind of a send-off,' said an elderly man at Edwin's side, 'and I think he'd like to think of us here drinking sherry.' He put down his empty glass and took another.

'People always say that,' said a woman who had joined them. 'And it's certainly convenient to suppose that anything we do is what *they* would have liked. But Matthew never entered a church in his life, so perhaps the drinking would be all he'd approve of.'

'I expect he was baptized and attended church when he was young,' Edwin observed, but the others moved away from him, making him feel that he had gone too far, not only by this observation but by attending the service at all. Yet he was undeniably a member of the staff, even if only a humble one, and had as much right as anyone to be paying his tribute to a man he had never known personally.

Edwin drained his glass and put it down carefully on the table. He noticed that it had been covered with a white cloth and wondered idly if it was of ecclesiastical significance. He decided not to help himself to another glass although he could easily have done so. It might not be fitting. Also a thing like that 'might get back' – you never knew.

Now the problem of lunch presented itself. Edwin had a sandwich in the office but he was not quite ready to face the others, so decided to go to a coffee house in Southampton Row, where he sat brooding in a curtained alcove, drinking strong Brazilian coffee.

A pair of lovers sat opposite him but he did not notice them. He was thinking about his own funeral – he would hardly rate a 'Memorial Service' – a proper Requiem, of course, with orange candles and incense and all the proper ceremonial details. He wondered if Father G. would outlive him and what hymns he would choose . . . A clock struck two and he realized that he ought to be getting back.

Norman looked up sourly as Edwin entered the room. Something had apparently 'come up' and Norman was having to deal with it.

'Nice work if you can get it – going to a Memorial Service at twelve and staying out three hours,' Norman commented.

'Two hours, twelve minutes,' said Edwin, consulting his watch. 'You could have come too if you'd wanted to.'

'Was it a beautiful service?' Letty asked. As an infrequent churchgoer she had the impression that services of this type were always beautiful.

'I wouldn't say that exactly,' said Edwin, hanging up his overcoat on a peg.

Marcia caught a mingled whiff of coffee and alcohol as he passed her to go to his table. 'What've you been up to?' she asked, but did not expect an answer.

Twelve

THE ORGANIZATION WHERE Letty and Marcia worked regarded it as a duty to provide some kind of a retirement party for them, when the time came for them to give up working. Their status as ageing unskilled women did not entitle them to an evening party, but it was felt that a lunchtime gathering, leading only to more than usual drowsiness in the afternoon, would be entirely appropriate. The other advantage of a lunchtime party was that only medium Cyprus sherry need be provided, whereas the evening called for more exotic and expensive drinks, wines and even the occasional carefully concealed bottle of whisky or gin – 'the hard stuff', as Norman called it, in his bitterness at being denied access to it. Also at lunchtime sandwiches could be eaten, so that there was no need to have lunch and it was felt by some that at a time like this it was 'better' to be eating – it gave one something to do.

Retirement was a serious business, to be regarded with respect, though the idea of it was incomprehensible to most of the staff. It was a condition that must be studied and prepared for, certainly – 'researched' they would have said – indeed it had already been the subject of a seminar, though the conclusions reached and the recommendations drawn up had no real bearing on the retirement of Letty and Marcia, which seemed as inevitable as the falling of the leaves in autumn, for which no kind of preparation needed to be made. If the two women feared that the coming of this date might give some clue to their ages, it was not an occasion for embarrassment because nobody else had been in the least interested, both of them having long ago reached ages beyond any kind of speculation. Each would be given a small golden handshake, but the state would provide for their basic needs which could not be all that great. Elderly women did not need much to eat, warmth was more necessary than food, and people like Letty and Marcia probably had either private means or savings, a nest-egg in the post office or a building society. It was comforting to think on these lines, and even if they had nothing extra, the social services were so much better now, there was no need for anyone to starve or freeze. And if governments failed in their duty there were always the media – continual goadings on television programmes, upsetting articles in the Sunday papers and disturbing pictures in the colour supplements. There was no need to worry about Miss Crowe and Miss Ivory.

The (acting) deputy assistant director, who had been commanded to make the presentation speech, wasn't quite sure what it was that Miss Crowe and Miss Ivory did or had done during their working lives. The activities of their department seemed to be shrouded in mystery – something to do with records or filing, it was thought, nobody knew for certain, but it was evidently 'women's work', the kind of thing that could easily be replaced by a computer. The most significant thing about it was that nobody was replacing them, indeed the whole department was being phased out and only being kept on until the men working in it reached retirement age. Yet under the influence of a quick swig of sherry, even this unpromising material could be used to good effect.

The deputy assistant director stepped into the middle of the room and began to speak.

'The point about Miss Crowe and Miss Ivory, whom we are met together to honour today, is that nobody knows exactly, or has ever known exactly, what it is that they do,' he declared boldly. 'They have been – they are – the kind of people who work quietly and secretly, doing good by stealth, as it were. Good, do I hear you ask? Yes, good, I repeat, and good I mean. In these days of industrial unrest it is people like Miss Ivory and Miss Crowe' – the names seemed to have got reversed, but presumably it didn't matter – 'who are an example to us all. We shall miss them very much, so much so that nobody has been found to replace them, but we would be the last to deny them the rewards of a well-earned retirement. It gives me much pleasure on behalf of the company and staff to present each of these ladies with a small token of our appreciation of their long and devoted service, which carries with it our best wishes for their future.'

Letty and Marcia then came forward, each to receive an envelope containing a cheque and a suitably inscribed card, the presenter remembered a luncheon engagement and slipped away, glasses were refilled and a buzz of talk broke out. Conversation had to be made and it did not come very easily once the obvious topics had been exhausted. As the party went on, people divided most easily into everyday working groups. It was the most natural thing then for Letty and Marcia to find themselves with Edwin and Norman, and for the latter to make some comment on the speech and to suggest that from what had been said he supposed they would spend their retirement setting the motor industry to rights.

Marcia was glad to be with people she knew. When she met other members of the staff she was conscious of her breastlessness, feeling that they must sense her imperfection, her incompleteness. Yet on the other hand she liked to talk about herself, to bring the conversation round to hospitals and surgeons, to pronounce in a lowered, reverent tone the name of Mr Strong. She could even, if it came to that, take some pleasure in saying 'my mastectomy' – it was the word 'breast' and the idea of it that upset her. None of the speeches and conversations dealing with her retirement had contained any references to breast (hope springing eternal in the human) or bosom (sentiments to which every b. returns an echo), as they might well have done had the deputy assistant director's speech been more literary.

It was of course generally known that Miss Ivory had undergone a serious operation, but the dress she was wearing today – a rather bright hyacinth blue courtelle – was several sizes too big for her skinny figure, so that very little of her shape was visible. People at the party who did not know her were fascinated by her strange appearance, that dyed hair and the peering beady eyes, and she might have provided unusual entertainment if one had had the courage to attempt a conversation with her. But one never did have quite that sort of courage when it came to the point. Ageing, slightly mad and on the threshold of retirement, it was an uneasy combination and it was no wonder that people shied away from her or made only the most perfunctory remarks. It was difficult to imagine what her retirement would be like – impossible and rather gruesome to speculate on it.

Letty, by contrast, was boringly straightforward. Even her rather nice green-patterned jersey suit and her newly set mousy hair were perfectly in character. She had already been classified as a typical English spinster about to retire to a cottage in the country, where she would be joining with others like her to engage in church activities, attending meetings of the Women's Institute, and doing gardening and needlework. People at the party therefore talked to her about all these things and Letty's natural modesty and politeness prevented her from telling them that she was no longer going to share a country cottage with a friend but would probably be spending the rest of her life in London. She knew that she was not a very interesting person, so she did not go into too much boring detail with the young people who enquired graciously about her future plans. Even Eulalia, the black junior, gave her an unexpectedly radiant smile. Another, whose thick, smooth straight neck rose up like a column of alabaster, the kind of girl it was impossible to imagine engaging in any of the mundane office jobs like typing or filing, suggested brightly that she'd be able to watch the telly in the afternoons, and Letty began to realize that things like this were, after all, one of the chief joys of retirement. She could not admit to this kind girl that she hadn't even got a television set.

Inevitably everyone had to get back to work and eventually Letty and Marcia found themselves in their own office with Edwin and Norman.

The two men seemed pleased with themselves. In their time they had attended a good many retirement parties and this one apparently came up to the standard which was measured by the number of times the sherry bottle went round.

'Of course sherry's a bit livery midday,' said Norman, 'but it's better than nothing. It does have its effect.' He swayed slightly in a comic manner.

'I find two glasses quite enough,' said Letty, 'and I think my glass must have been refilled when I wasn't looking because I feel quite . . .' She didn't really know how she felt or how to describe it; she was certainly not drunk but neither tiddly nor tipsy seemed suitably dignified.

Marcia, who had taken nothing but a small glass of orange juice, gave a tight-lipped smile.

'At least you won't have a drinking problem when you retire,' Norman teased.

'I hate the stuff,' she declared.

Letty found herself thinking about the lonely evenings ahead of her in Mrs Pope's silent house. Perhaps it would be as well not to have a bottle of sherry in her room … She had got on quite well with Mrs Pope so far, when she was out all day, but would it be the same when she retired? Obviously the arrangement could only be temporary. One did not relish the idea of spending the rest of one's life in a north-west London suburb. There was no reason why she shouldn't find a room in a village somewhere near where Marjorie and her husband would be living – Marjorie had hinted in her last letter that she would welcome something of the kind, she didn't want to lose touch after all these years … Or she might go back to the west of England where she was born. She told herself, dutifully assuming the suggested attitude towards retirement, that life was still full of possibilities.

Letty began clearing out her office drawer, neatly arranging its contents in her shopping bag. There was not much to be taken away – a pair of light slippers for the days when she needed to change her shoes, a box of paper handkerchiefs, writing paper and envelopes, a packet of indigestion tablets. Following Letty's example, Marcia began to do the same, muttering as she did so and stuffing the contents into a large carrier bag. Letty knew that Marcia's drawer was very full although she had never seen inside it properly, only caught glimpses of things bulging out when Marcia opened it. She knew that there was a pair of exercise sandals in which Marcia used to clump around in the days when she had first bought them, but she was surprised to see her take out several tins of food – meat, beans and soups.

'Quite a gourmet feast you've got there,' Norman remarked. 'If only we'd known.'

Marcia smiled but said nothing. Norman seemed to be able to get away with these teasing comments, Letty thought. She had turned aside, not wanting to see what Marcia was taking out of the drawer. It seemed an intrusion into Marcia's private life, something it was better not to know about.

'It will seem funny without you both,' said Edwin awkwardly.

He did not really know what to say now that it had come to the point. None of them knew, for it was the kind of occasion that seemed to demand something more than the usual goodbye or goodnight of the end of an ordinary working day. Perhaps they should have given the women a present of some kind – but *what*? He and Norman had discussed it, but decided in the end that it was altogether too difficult. 'They wouldn't expect it – it would only embarrass them,' they had concluded, 'and it's not as if we were never going to see them again.' In the circumstances it was much easier to assume this but without going into too much detail about it. For of course they would all meet again – Letty and Marcia would revisit the office, 'pop in' some time. There might even be meetings outside the office – a kind of get-together for lunch or 'something' . . . even if it was beyond imagining what that something might be, at least it made it easier for them all to go on their separate ways assuming a vague future together.

Thirteen

'YOU'LL BE RETIRING,' Janice Brabner had said. 'Have you thought at all what you're going to do?'

'Do?' Marcia stared at her blankly. 'What do you mean?'

'Well . . .' Janice faltered but, as she afterwards recounted, pressed on regardless. 'You'll have a good deal of time on your hands, won't you – time that you gave to your job?' Marcia had never revealed what exactly her job was but Janice guessed that it hadn't been particularly exciting. After all, what kind of job could somebody like Marcia do? She wished she wouldn't keep staring at her in that unnerving way, as if she had no idea what was meant by Janice asking what she was going to do when she retired.

'A woman can always find plenty to occupy her time,' Marcia said at last. 'It isn't like a man retiring, you know. I have my house to see to.'

'Yes, of course.' And it could do with seeing to, Janice thought. But was Marcia capable of doing what was necessary? Physically she seemed able to do housework so that there was no question of getting a home help for her, even if one could be found, but keeping a house in order needed a certain attitude of mind and it was here that Marcia seemed to be lacking. Did she not notice the dust or care about it? Perhaps she needed new spectacles – a word here might be in order ... Janice sighed, as she so often did when considering Marcia. There seemed to be nothing she could do at the moment beyond keeping an eye on her and calling in occasionally to see how she was coping.

The first Monday morning Marcia woke at the usual time and began getting up and preparing to leave the house before she remembered that it was the first day of her retirement. 'Roll on,' people used to say in those days when it had seemed an impossibly remote event, as unlikely as winning the pools or having your number come up on Ernie. Well, now it had rolled on, it was here. A woman can always find plenty to occupy her time.

Marcia took down the tray she had used for her early morning tea, but she left the cup behind on the dressing table where it would remain for some days, the dregs of milky tea eventually separating into sourness. As she was not going to the office, she changed the dress she had put on for her old Saturday morning skirt and a crumpled blouse which needed ironing, but there was nobody to notice it or to criticize and no doubt the warmth of her body would soon press out the creases. Downstairs at the sink she was about to wash up yesterday's dishes when she was diverted by the sight of a plastic bag lying on the kitchen table. How had that got there and what had been in it? So many things seemed to come in plastic bags now that it was difficult to keep track of them. The main thing was not to throw it away carelessly, better still to put it away in a safe place, because there was a note printed on it which read 'To avoid danger of suffocation keep this wrapper away from babies and children'. They could have said from middle-aged and elderly persons too, who might well have an irresistible urge to suffocate themselves. So Marcia took the bag upstairs into what had been the spare bedroom where she kept things like cardboard boxes, brown paper and string, and stuffed it into a drawer already bulging with other plastic bags, conscientiously kept away from babies and children. It was a very long time since any such had entered the house, children not for many years, babies perhaps never.

Marcia spent a long time in the room, tidying and rearranging its contents. All the plastic bags needed to be taken out of the drawer and sorted into their different shapes and sizes, classified as it were. It was something she had been meaning to do for such a long time but somehow she had never seemed to have a moment. Now, the first day of her retirement, she had eternity stretching before her. It amused her to remember Janice Brabner asking in that rather mincing, refined voice of hers, 'Have you thought at all what you're going to do?'

The task took until what would in the office have been lunchtime and Marcia did wonder for a moment what Edwin and Norman would be doing, but of course it would be just what they always did, eating whatever lunch they had brought with them, Edwin with his finicky things and Norman making himself coffee from the big shared tin she had left behind. Then Edwin visiting some church to see what was going on there and Norman perhaps strolling as far as the British Museum to sit in front of the mummified animals. Or perhaps he wouldn't get any further than the library and a look at the papers, and thinking of the library reminded her that she still hadn't done anything about that milk bottle which Letty had foisted on her. If the worst came to the worst she could always leave it at the library, or any library, as she wouldn't be going to that particular one any more . . .

Marcia gave no thought to her own lunch and it was evening before she had anything to eat and then only a cup of tea and the remains of one of the bits of bread she found in the bread bin. She did not notice the greenish mould fringing the crust, but she wasn't hungry anyway and only ate half the slice, putting the remainder back for future consumption. Of course she would go out shopping some time, perhaps tomorrow, but not today even though the Indian shop would still be open. There were plenty of bits and pieces to finish up and she had never been a big eater.

Letty had imagined herself sleeping late on that first morning, but she woke up at the usual time, in fact earlier because Mrs Pope was up at six o'clock and clattering out of the house, no doubt to observe some obscure saint's day with a service at the church. Letty would probably have woken up anyway, so strong was the habit of forty years. And older people are said to wake up earlier, she thought, so perhaps the habit would never be broken.

'What are you going to *do* when you retire?' people had asked her, some in a genuine spirit of enquiry, others with ghoulish curiosity. And naturally she had made the usual answers – how nice it would be not to have to go to the office – how she would now have time to do all those things she had always wanted to do (these 'things' were unspecified) – and read all the books she had never had time to read before – *Middlemarch* and *War and Peace,* perhaps even *Dr Zhivago*. And really, when it came to retiring, she could have said, as Marcia had, 'A woman can always find plenty to occupy her time' – that was the great thing, being a woman. It was men one felt sorry for in retirement. Of course in one respect she was different from Marcia, she had no house to see to, only this room in another woman's house, and there was a limit to what one could do in it or to it. All the more opportunity to devote herself to some serious reading, and that would mean a visit to the library. It would be good to get out on this first morning, to have an object for a walk.

By the time Letty had decided to go down to the kitchen to get her breakfast, Mrs Pope had come back from church. She was very brisk and virtuous. It was a chilly morning but the walk had done her good. There had been three people at the early service, five if one counted the priest and his server. Letty did not know what comment to make, for she had always understood from Edwin that these very early services were rather old-fashioned now and that an evening Mass was the thing. Still, the thought of Edwin gave her a conversational opening and she was able to ask Mrs Pope about his connection with her church.

'Oh, he's not a regular member of our congregation – he only comes if there's something special going on,' Mrs Pope said, fiercely scraping a piece of burnt toast.

'We're not nearly high enough for him – no incense, you see.'

'No incense?' Again Letty was at a loss.

'It doesn't agree with everyone, you know. If you're at all bronchial ... Do you not get dressed for breakfast, Miss Crowe?'

Letty, who had come down to the kitchen in her respectable blue woollen housecoat, felt that she was being criticized. 'It's the first day of my retirement,' she explained, feebly, she felt, as if that was enough justification.

'But I think you will find it better not to allow yourself to get slack. So many people go to pieces in retirement – I've seen it so often. A man may be in a responsible position, then he retires ...'

'But I am a woman and I was not at all in a responsible position,' Letty reminded her. 'And this morning I'm going to the library – I shall at last have time to do some serious reading.'

'Oh, reading ...' Mrs Pope did not seem to have much use for reading, and the conversation, if it had been that, languished. Mrs Pope had gone to church fasting and now prepared to enjoy her bacon and scraped toast, while Letty went back to her room with a boiled egg and two slices of crispbread.

Later she dressed, more carefully than Marcia had done on her first day of retirement. It was an opportunity to wear a new tweed suit which had been considered too good for the office, and to spend more time than usual in choosing the jumper and scarf to go with it. So far her day was being different, but when it came to the next part of it she realized that she would be going to the library near the office where she had a reader's ticket, and that the journey to it would be the one she had taken every day. But now, two hours later, the train was less crowded and when she got out at her station people let themselves be carried up on the escalator rather than walking up.

To reach the library she had to pass the office, and naturally she glanced up at the grey monolithic building and wondered what Edwin and Norman were doing up there on the third floor. It was not too difficult to picture them at coffee time, and at least there would be nobody installed in her and Marcia's places, doing their work, since nobody was to replace them. It seemed to Letty that what cannot now be justified has perhaps never existed, and it gave her the feeling that she and Marcia had been swept away as if they had never been. With this sensation of nothingness she entered the library. The young male assistant with the shoulder-length golden hair was still in his place, so that at least was reassuring. Confidently she went over to the sociology shelves, determined to begin on her serious reading. The idea and the name 'social studies' had attracted her and she was eager to find out what it was all about.

'I wonder what the girls are doing now,' said Norman.

'The girls?' Of course Edwin knew perfectly well whom he meant but he was not used to talking or thinking of Letty and Marcia in this way.

'A nice lie-in, then breakfast in bed, elevenses in town and a wander round the shops – lunch in Dickins & Jones, perhaps, or D. H. Evans. Then back home well before the rush hour, then I...' Norman's imagination failed at this point and Edwin was not capable of filling in the gaps.

'That's quite likely for Letty,' he said, 'but I can't see Marcia spending her day like that.'

'No, she wouldn't want to go round the shops,' said Norman thoughtfully. 'Letty was the one who used to go to Oxford Street in the lunch hour – didn't even mind waiting for a bus.'

'No – we sometimes used to meet in the queue when I was going to All Saints, Margaret Street.'

'You never persuaded her to join you,' said Norman sardonically.

Edwin seemed embarrassed, almost as if he had tried and failed, but Norman did not press the point. 'It seems funny without them,' he said.

'Perhaps they'll pop in some time,' Edwin suggested.

'Yes, they did say they'd pop in.'

'Not that I can really imagine them doing that – they'd have to come up in the lift, wouldn't they, and that's not quite the same.'

'Not as if we were on the ground floor and could be seen from the street,' said Norman, almost wistfully.

'At least we've got a bit more room now.' Edwin began to arrange his lunch on what had been Letty's table, spreading out slices of bread, a tub of polyunsaturated margarine, cheese and tomatoes. Taking out a packet of jelly babies he had a sudden and vivid picture of Letty, but why this should have materialized at this particular moment and with such intensity he could not have said. Surely nothing to do with the jelly babies?

It had been a long day and in a curious way a tiring one, as tiring as a working day, Letty felt. Perhaps it had been the early waking and the longer than usual evening, beginning with a period between tea and supper which she did not remember as having existed before. She had made a determined effort to read one of the books she had brought from the library, but it had been heavy going.

Obviously it would take some time to acquire the knack of serious reading and perhaps it would be better to go on with it in the morning when she was feeling fresher.

Marcia's day seemed to have gone in a flash, though speed was not a concept in her life. She had no sense of time passing and was surprised when darkness came. Her most conscious thought was irritation at the idea that the do-gooding social worker might call, so she did not put the light on but sat in darkness, listening to the mindless chatter and atavistic noise of Radio I turned down low. She had no memory of having experienced the first day of her retirement.

Fourteen

LETTY HAD BEEN retired for a week and had drawn the first payment of her pension before she found herself coming to the conclusion that sociology was not quite all that she had hoped for. Perhaps she had chosen the wrong books, for surely 'social studies' must be more interesting than this? She had imagined herself revelling and wallowing – perhaps these words were too violent to describe what she had imagined – in her chosen subject, not frozen with boredom, baffled and bogged down by incomprehensible jargon, continually looking at her watch to see if it could be time to make a cup of coffee. It must be that she was too old to learn anything new and that her brain had become atrophied. Had she indeed ever had a brain? Going back over her past life, she found it difficult to remember anything she had ever done that required brain work, certainly not the job from which she had just retired. She seemed to be totally unfitted for academic work, yet people older than she was were taking courses at the Open University. Mrs Pope knew a woman in her seventies who was in her second year. But Mrs Pope, it seemed, always knew somebody who was doing something wholly admirable, and as time went on Letty found herself avoiding her and choosing to cook her meals when she knew that Mrs Pope would not be using the kitchen.

She would crouch in her room listening for sounds, trying to detect the smell of cooking, though this was often difficult as Mrs Pope seldom had anything fried except bacon. Letty would find herself pouring a second glass of sherry while she waited for Mrs Pope to leave the kitchen. But she still kept to her rules – one did not drink sherry before the evening, just as one did not read a novel in the morning, this last being a left-over dictum of a headmistress of forty years ago.

When the sociology books were due to be returned to the library, Letty took them back, feeling guilty and dissatisfied. But you were supposed to enjoy retirement, at least the first weeks of it. Have a good rest, do all those things you've always wanted to do, people had said. Why shouldn't she just read novels and listen to the radio and knit and think about her clothes? She wondered what Marcia was doing, how she was getting on. It was a pity she wasn't on the telephone for it would have been so much easier to have a chat or arrange a meeting that way.

'You could travel,' people had said and Letty had to agree with them, though it was not easy to imagine the kind of travelling she would do, alone on a package tour now that Marjorie was so much occupied with David Lydell. Listening to a phone-in programme on the radio she had heard a question about holidays for people on their own, and the answer conjuring up a picture of a crowd of congenial middle-aged and elderly people of both sexes with interests in common – botany and archaeology or even 'wine' (as opposed to solitary drinking). In the end her courage failed her and she got no further than studying the brochure, like Norman diving for buried treasure in Greece. Her attempts at 'travel' ended in a weekend visit to a distant cousin living in the West Country town where she had been born.

The cousin, a woman of about Letty's age, was friendly and welcoming and they sat cosily knitting together in the evenings. Letty had long since accustomed herself to being without a man in her life and, as a result of this lack, to having no children. The cousin was a widow and did not make Letty feel in any way inadequate. All the same, it was when she was staying here that Letty began to realize another way in which she had failed. It was not something that had previously occurred to her, but looking through the cousin's photograph album she saw clearly what it was – she had no grandchildren! That was it. How could she ever have imagined such a thing, all those years ago?

Returning from her weekend, she thought again of getting in touch with Marcia. She decided to write her a note, suggesting that they might meet for lunch or tea in town. It was perhaps a little early to compare notes about their retirement but at least they could talk about old times at the office.

Janice's next visit to Marcia was some weeks after her retirement – time for her to have settled down and to have worked out some kind of a pattern for her days, Janice thought. No doubt she missed the companionship of the office – 'they', the retired ones, often mentioned that – and the routine that even a boring occupation provides. Still, as Marcia herself had said, a woman can always find plenty to occupy her time and she had her house to see to. She had a garden, too, and that could have done with a bit of attention, Janice considered, as she waited on the doorstep and contemplated the dusty laurels whose overgrown foliage almost concealed the downstairs front window.

When Marcia reluctantly opened the door to admit her, Janice was startled by the change in her appearance. It was some seconds before she realized what the difference was. Since her retirement, Marcia had not bothered to touch up the roots of her hair which now stood out snowy white against the stiff, dark brown of the rest. Perhaps she was deliberately letting the dye grow out so that she might achieve the soft white curls of the majority of the pensioners visited by Janice, though, knowing Marcia, this seemed doubtful. She really ought to have the dyed part cut out, creating a short neat style of the white part, as many elderly people did. Janice wondered if she could tactfully convey the information about reduced charges for pensioners at some of the local hairdressers. But why bother to be all that tactful? You had to be a bit forthright with people like Marcia, and there was no time like the present.

'I suppose you do know that you can get your hair done at a reduced price at Marietta's if you go between nine and twelve on Mondays and Tuesdays?' Janice said, in her sweetest manner. So many of them don't *know* what they're entitled to, how people are *falling over backwards* to help them, was the social workers' wail.

'I got a leaflet from the library telling me all that sort of thing,' said Marcia impatiently, and Janice felt that she was being dismissed.

'Don't forget that you can always come along to the Centre,' she said, going out of the front door. 'We get quite a lot of retired people there and they seem to like to have a chat with others in the same boat.' Perhaps that hadn't been the happiest way of putting it, and really it was rather comic, the picture of all these retired people in some kind of boat. Sometimes you almost felt it wouldn't be a bad idea to shove them off all together somewhere. Tony, Janice's husband, used to joke about it but of course old people were no joking matter, as she kept reminding herself. And Marcia hadn't smiled at the idea of the boat, hadn't even replied to the suggestion that she might go along to the Centre. Janice sighed.

Marcia watched her getting into her car and driving away. Young people couldn't walk a step these days, she thought. And what was all that about hairdressers? Janice's own hair was streaked all different colours, so she couldn't talk. Marcia didn't like going to the hairdresser, anyway, she hadn't been for years. Not like Letty, who went every week. No doubt *she* would be taking advantage of the reduced charges for pensioners ... Marcia stood in the hall, a feeling of dissatisfaction creeping over her at the idea of Letty. It was that business of the milk bottle, chiefly, but there was something else too. Letty had sent her a postcard, suggesting that they might meet some time – as if she would want to do that! There was no knowing what Letty might foist on her, given the chance. She was certainly going to ignore the card.

Letty had expected some kind of an answer from Marcia to her suggestion of a meeting, but she was not altogether surprised when none came. One could very quickly grow away from people and that life at the office, where they had never been close friends, now seemed utterly remote. Instead, though it was in no way comparable, she received a letter from Marjorie, announcing that she was coming to London to do some shopping and asking Letty to have lunch with her.

They met in the restaurant of an Oxford Street store, rather as Norman had pictured Letty lunching on her first day of retirement. It appeared that Marjorie had come to London to buy clothes for her trousseau, which seemed to Letty not only an old-fashioned idea but an inappropriate one for a woman in her sixties. Yet Marjorie had always been of a romantic nature, getting the most out of unpromising circumstances. Even Marcia, Letty recalled, had an 'interest' in the surgeon who had performed her operation, so that a visit to hospital was something to be looked forward to. Only Letty, it seemed, was without romance in her life, and the prospect of Marjorie's marriage was something beyond her imagining. If she had now got over any disappointment she may have felt at the cancellation of her retirement plans, she was still not able to enter fully into Marjorie's rapture. But she could offer suggestions about clothes and perhaps that was something.

'I shall be wearing a blue crêpe dress,' Marjorie was saying, 'and I thought of getting a small, matching hat.'

'You could wear a wide-brimmed hat,' Letty said. A woman of their age could do with a few becoming shadows cast on the face, she thought.

'Oh, do you think so? Yes, I suppose it's not like Royalty – people don't necessarily expect to see one's face – or want to,' Marjorie laughed. 'And of course there won't be crowds of people – it's going to be very quiet.'

'Yes, I suppose so.' The weddings of older people usually were.

'You don't mind, do you, Letty?'

'Mind?' Letty was surprised at the question.

'At not being asked to be a bridesmaid, I mean.'

'Of course not! I never thought of it.' Older women attending each other in this way seemed highly unsuitable and she was surprised that Marjorie had suggested it. In any case, Letty had been a bridesmaid at Marjorie's first wedding. She wondered if Marjorie had forgotten this but was too tactful to remind her of it.

'And we shan't even be having any guests – just my brother to give me away and a friend of David's, a fellow priest, as best man.'

'Has he any relations?'

'Just his mother – he's an only child.'

'But his mother won't be at the wedding?'

Marjorie smiled. 'Well, she's in her ninetieth year, so I would hardly expect it. She is living in a religious community – the nuns have taken her in.'

'To end her days? It seems a good arrangement.' Letty saw that churchgoing might have some unexpected advantages and wondered if Mrs Pope had arranged to be taken in by nuns one day.

'And how are things with you, Letty?' said Marjorie, when there was a pause in the conversation. 'You like your new arrangement – the room in NW6. Hampstead, is it?'

'Well, more West Hampstead,' Letty admitted. If it had been genuine Hampstead she would have said so.

'I still think you might have been happier at Holmhurst in the village, as I suggested. I could still put your name down, you know. There's sure to be a vacancy in the near future.'

'Yes, you said that before – somebody might die – but I suppose that vacancy has been filled now.'

'Oh, yes – but somebody else is sure to die – it's happening all the time,' said Marjorie brightly.

They had some coffee and Letty said that she thought she would stay where she was for the time being.

'Yes, it does seem very satisfactory,' said Marjorie, who obviously wanted to find it so. 'Mrs Pope seems a splendid sort of woman.'

'Yes, she is wonderful for her age,' said Letty, repeating what people always said about her. 'She's very active in the parish. I suppose you'll have to be that when you're married.'

'Oh, I shall enjoy it. To be able to *help* somebody, don't you think that's the main purpose of life, what everybody...' Marjorie hesitated and Letty realized that she did not like to go further, to emphasize the contrast between her own enviable position, that of being a helpmate to a man, and Letty's state of useless retirement.

'I sometimes think I ought to get another job,' Letty said, 'part time, perhaps.'

'Oh, don't be in too much of a hurry to do that,' said Marjorie quickly, unwilling to give up the luxury of having a friend less useful than herself. 'Enjoy your leisure and all the things you can do now. If only I had time to do some serious reading, I often think.'

Letty remembered the books on social studies which she had returned to the library, but Marjorie was already on to another subject – a pair of warm bedroom slippers for her future husband.

Should they go to Austin Reed's? As they walked out of the restaurant together, Letty contemplated the ample shape of her friend and wondered where in all these years she, Letty, had failed.

Fifteen

'IT'S NOT THE money,' Norman was saying. 'Goodness knows, I don't grudge the old dears a lunch.'

Edwin noted that Letty and Marcia, previously 'the girls', were now 'the old dears'. Neither description seemed entirely suitable, but as he had nothing better to add he made no comment. 'We did say we'd keep in touch,' he reminded Norman, 'and they've been gone some time now.'

'Yes, time to've settled down – it was best to leave it for a bit. Of course we could use luncheon vouchers, if we went to the Rendezvous, that is.'

'Luncheon vouchers? Do you think so? It doesn't seem very . . .' Edwin hesitated.

'Gracious, you mean? You don't imagine it's going to be a *gracious* occasion, do you?' Norman was at his most sarcastic. 'That was what I meant – just the whole idea of it, not the money. I'm quite willing to fork out 50p for their lunches.'

'I think you'll have to fork out a good deal more than 50p,' said Edwin, 'though we could use some luncheon vouchers. I've got quite a few saved up and after all they'd never know. You pay at the cash desk at the Rendezvous, so one of us could do the necessary without them seeing.'

'It's the awkwardness,' Norman went on. 'We've never had a restaurant meal with them before. Can you see the four of us sitting at a table?'

'You're not suggesting we should have sandwiches in the office? They'd hardly thank us for that.'

'But what are we going to talk about, once we've asked them how they are and all that?'

'Oh, we'll manage,' said Edwin, with a confidence he did not altogether feel, though he was so used to sticky church occasions that a lunch with two former colleagues should have been well within his powers. And after all, it had been his idea to invite Letty and Marcia to lunch. His conscience had been nagging at him and in the end he had written to them – in office time, of course, as it really counted as 'work' – extending the invitation. Letty had replied promptly, saying that she would very much like to see them again. Marcia's answer had taken longer to come and her acceptance gave the impression of conveying a favour, for she was so very busy. Edwin and Norman wondered what she could be doing that kept her so occupied. Perhaps she had taken another job, unlikely though this seemed.

'Anyway, we shall soon know,' said Edwin, as the time drew near. He had heard from Mrs Pope at the church (he had gone over for their dedication festival) that Letty seemed to have settled down well but that she was inclined to 'keep herself to herself', as if this was a bad thing. Nobody had heard any news of Marcia since her retirement, though Edwin occasionally passed the end of the road where she lived and had more than once thought of calling on her unexpectedly. But something, he wasn't sure what, had always held him back. The parable of the good Samaritan kept coming into his mind and making him feel uncomfortable, though it wasn't in the least appropriate. There was no question of him 'passing by on the other side' when he didn't even go anywhere near the house, and for all they knew, Marcia was perfectly happy.

Of course Edwin did not know that she was, but for some obscure reason he felt that if anyone was to blame for not having kept in touch it was Norman.

It had been arranged that Letty and Marcia should come to the office and that they should all go on to lunch from there. Letty was the first to arrive, wearing her best tweed suit and carrying a new pair of gloves. 'So nice not to have to bother with a shopping bag,' she said, her eyes taking in not only Edwin and Norman, who appeared very much the same, but the changes that had taken place in the room.

'I see you've spread yourselves out a bit,' she said, noticing that the men now seemed to occupy all the space that had once accommodated the four of them. Again she experienced the feeling of nothingness, when it was borne in on her so forcibly that she and Marcia had been phased out in this way, as if they had never existed. Looking round the room, her eyes lighted on a spider plant which she had brought one day and not bothered to take away when she left. It had proliferated; many little offshoots were now hanging down until they dangled over the radiator. Was there some significance in this, a proof that she had once existed, that the memory of her lingered on? At least nature went on, whatever happened to us; she knew that.

'Yes, it's grown, that plant,' Edwin said. 'I've watered it every week.'

'You left a bit of yourself behind,' said Norman, in his chatty way, but then, as if by mutual consent, they left the subject, each perhaps fearing a deeper significance. 'Marcia knows the time we arranged?' Norman asked sharply. 'It's best to go early to get a table.'

'Yes, I said 12.30, and it must be nearly that now,' said Edwin. 'Is that someone at the door now?'

It was Marcia, making something of an entrance because of her strange appearance.

When she had received the invitation from Edwin she had at first told herself that it was 'out of the question' – she could not possibly spare the time to come up to town for lunch. Then it occurred to her that it would be a golden opportunity to return the alien milk bottle to Letty, so she wrapped it in plastic and put it in her shopping bag. Unlike Letty she had brought one with her, as she intended to go to Sainsbury's to replenish her supply of tinned foods.

It took the others a moment or two to recover from the apparition standing before them. Marcia was thinner than ever and her light-coloured summer coat hung on her emaciated body. On her feet she wore old fur-lined sheepskin boots and a pair of much darned stockings, and on her head an unsuitably jaunty straw hat from which her strangely piebald hair straggled in elflocks.

Edwin, who was not particularly observant, did realize that she was wearing an odd assortment of garments but did not think she looked much different from usual. Norman thought, poor old girl, obviously going round the bend. Letty, as a clothes-conscious woman, was appalled – that anyone could get to the stage of caring so little about her appearance, of not even noticing how she looked, made her profoundly uneasy and almost conscience-stricken, as if she ought to have done something more about Marcia in her retirement. But then of course she *had* suggested a meeting and Marcia hadn't answered her letter . . . And now she was made to feel ashamed because she felt embarrassed at the idea of sitting in a restaurant with Marcia.

Luckily the Rendezvous was fairly empty and they found a table in a secluded corner.

'This place lives up to its name for once,' said Norman, making bright conversation as they studied the menu. 'It really is a rendezvous for . . .' He did not say 'friends', for they were not exactly that, and 'colleagues' sounded too formal and slightly ridiculous.

'A meeting place for people who haven't seen each other for some time,' Letty suggested, and the men were grateful to her; but she had not seen it like this in the days when she used to lunch alone here. It had always seemed full of solitary people eating lonely meals.

'Now, what are we going to eat?' said Edwin, turning especially to Marcia who looked most in need of food, or sustenance, one could almost say.

'You look as if you could do with a square meal,' said Norman bluntly. 'What about some soup to start off with and then the roast or chicken?'

'Oh, just a salad for me,' said Marcia. 'I never eat a heavy meal in the middle of the day.'

'Well, I think the rest of us will want more than that,' said Edwin heartily.

'Yes, it doesn't seem quite the weather for salads,' Letty agreed.

'I should've thought you'd be a salad enthusiast,' said Norman. 'You've put on a bit of weight, haven't you.' His tone was teasing but Letty detected the hint of malice in it. She knew that he was right, for since her retirement eating had been one of her main interests and enjoyments. 'Some elderly people do enjoy their food,' Norman went on, hardly improving matters, for even now Letty did not think of herself as elderly. 'Others couldn't care less.'

'Now come on, all of you,' said Edwin, who was conscious of the hovering waitress. 'What's it to be?'

In the end, Letty had the chicken 'forestière', Norman the roast pork and Edwin, whose vegetarianism did not exclude fish, the plaice and chips. Marcia was not to be 'tempted', as Norman put it, and insisted on a small cheese salad. When it came to drink, the men had lager while Letty was persuaded to take a glass of white wine. Marcia, of course, had nothing and made rather a feature of her abstinence, much to the amusement of two young men at the next table.

'Well now . . .' Edwin's relief at the safe arrival of the food was evident in his more relaxed manner, for as he had suggested it he regarded himself as responsible for the success of the enterprise. 'Everything to your satisfaction? Wouldn't you like a roll and butter with your salad?' he suggested to Marcia.

'I never eat bread with my meals,' she declared.

'You'll get so that you can't eat if you're not careful,' Norman pronounced. 'Anorexia nervosa, they call it – there was a talk about it on the radio.'

'It's young girls who get anorexia nervosa,' said Marcia, correcting him from her superior medical knowledge. 'I've never been a big eater.'

'I hope your chicken is all right?' said Edwin to Letty. As if *he* should care about Letty's food, he thought, amused at himself, but one had to play the host on this occasion.

'Thank you, it's quite delicious,' said Letty politely.

'Vegetables and that,' said Norman, 'I suppose that's what "forestière" means – things from the forest. Though you wouldn't really get vegetables in a forest, would you?'

'This has mushrooms in it,' said Letty, 'and you might certainly find those in a wood or forest.'

'But you wouldn't fancy them,' said Norman, 'not out of the forest.'

'Of course now most mushrooms are cultivated,' Edwin suggested. 'I believe it's quite a lucrative thing to take up in one's retirement.'

'Hardly in a bedsitter,' said Norman. 'You and Marcia could go in for it, though, in your houses, if you've got a basement or a shed in the garden.'

Marcia looked up at him suspiciously. 'My shed is used for quite another purpose,' she said.

'Dark secrets,' said Norman, but Marcia did not seem to be amused.

'I don't think Edwin was suggesting that any of us should go in for mushroom cultivation,' said Letty, 'though I believe people make quite a success of it.'

'Do you know of anyone who has gone in for it?' Edwin asked.

'Oh no,' said Letty hastily.

That seemed to kill off that particular topic of conversation and there was a short silence which was broken by Edwin asking what they would like to eat next, 'sweet, pudding or dessert, as the Americans say'.

'Nothing more for me, thank you,' said Marcia firmly. Having messed her salad about in an unattractive way, she had left most of it on the side of her plate.

Letty, remembering Norman's remark about her weight, decided that she might as well be hung for a sheep as a lamb and make the most of the meal. She could have a low-calorie supper tonight. 'I'd like apple pie and ice cream,' she said.

'Aunt Betsy's apple pie,' Norman pointed out. 'I think I'll have that too.'

Edwin decided to have caramel pudding and tried to persuade Marcia to change her mind, but he was unsuccessful.

'We haven't really asked what you two are doing with yourselves in your retirement,' Norman said, 'what you're getting up to.'

That way of putting it added a lighter touch and Letty told them about her efforts to take up social studies and her ignominious failure to get through the books.

'I don't wonder,' said Norman. 'You don't want to bother with that kind of thing. You want to get a good rest. After all the work you did here you deserve it.'

Letty wondered again what that work had been that it had left so little mark on anybody, and added, 'I seem to fill my time quite pleasantly.' She must never give the slightest hint of loneliness or boredom, the sense of time hanging heavy.

'What about that friend of yours – the one who was going to marry the vicar?' Edwin asked.

'Oh, she hasn't married him yet. I had lunch with her the other day.'

'I suppose there wouldn't be any hurry,' said Edwin, unconscious of any possibility of misunderstanding, which Norman seized on.

'I should hope not!' Norman said. 'And anyway, marry in haste and repent at leisure.'

'There surely wouldn't be any question of that,' said Edwin.

'Well, no,' Letty agreed. 'The saying doesn't really apply to people in their sixties.'

'It could apply,' said Norman, 'why not, indeed? And I think you told us that the lady is some years older than her intended.'

'Did I tell you? I don't remember that.' Letty hoped she had not been uncharitable about her friend.

'And what have you been doing with yourself?' Edwin turned to Marcia with an air of kindly enquiry which hardly deserved the fierceness of her reply.

'That's my business,' she snapped.

'Been to the hospital again?' Norman asked, humouring her. 'Still under the doctor, aren't you?'

Marcia mumbled the name of Mr Strong then, raising her voice, began to complain about the interfering visits of the social worker.

Letty drained the last drops of her wine with a feeling of regret. It had not been a very large glass. 'No social worker has ever visited me,' she said.

'You haven't had a major operation, have you,' said Marcia,

rather too loudly. The same young men at the next table were again amused.

'Well, that does say something for the National Health Service and the after-care,' said Edwin, 'that they should keep an eye on the people who've been in hospital. I find that very encouraging.'

'Don't tell us you're planning to have a major operation – the same one as Marcia had,' Norman joked.

There was a feeling that he had gone a little too far and Edwin hastily asked if he should order coffee for all of them.

'Not for me,' said Marcia, 'I really must be going. I have a lot of shopping to do.'

'Oh, stay till we've had ours,' said Norman, coaxing her. 'It isn't often we get the chance of a chat.'

A curious expression, which only Letty appeared to notice, came over Marcia's face. It could almost have been said that she softened. Had she some feeling for Norman, then? But it was only a momentary change, and while the others were drinking their coffee she was again impatient to go.

'I suppose you two ought to be getting back to the grindstone,' said Letty, when it seemed that the lunch hour could not be prolonged.

'If you can call it that,' said Edwin.

'It certainly seems like that sometimes,' said Norman. 'Roll on retirement.'

Letty wondered what he would do in his bed-sitting room when he retired, and had an impulse to talk to him about it, but of course there was no time for that kind of thing – work, or what passed for work, had to be done and the two men had already been out of the office longer than usual. Still, it was a special occasion, not the kind of thing that happened every day, and if they had been challenged Edwin and Norman would have been prepared to defend themselves. But nobody questioned them and they slipped back to their room unnoticed.

Marcia hurried into a side street where there was a small branch of Sainsbury's. As she delved into her shopping bag, preparing it to receive the various tins she intended to buy, her hand came upon the wrapped milk bottle she had forgotten to return to Letty. What a nuisance! For a moment she wondered if she could catch the others up but although she hurried back along the street they had gone too far and there was no sign of them. She turned away, frustrated.

When she reached Sainsbury's there was a curiously empty look about the building and nobody was coming out or going in. Had she forgotten that it might be early closing? But surely that was Saturday? She went nearer and peered in at the door. A shocking sight met her eyes – the place was swept and garnished, almost razed to the ground. It was indeed closed, and for ever, as from a date some weeks ago, and nobody had told her. That branch of Sainsbury's was abandoned, it was no more, and she could not buy the tins to take back for her store cupboard. Unreasonably, she blamed Edwin and Norman for not having informed her of the fact. There was nothing for it but to go to the library.

Letty, after leaving the two men, had gone in there too, and Marcia crept up behind her as she browsed among the biographies.

'This is yours, I think,' said Marcia in an accusing tone, thrusting the wrapped milk bottle towards her.

'A milk bottle?' Of course Letty did not remember the occasion and Marcia had to explain it which she did, loudly, so that other people turned round and the young blonde-haired library assistant seemed about to make some kind of protest.

Letty, conscious of tension in the air, accepted the bottle without further question, and Marcia walked away quickly, feeling that although coming up to town for lunch had been a waste of time, at least it had had a satisfactory outcome. Letty, encumbered with the bottle and having no shopping bag with her, left the library without choosing a book and deposited the bottle in a crate outside the grocer's shop near the office. Marcia could perfectly well have done this herself, she reflected, but obviously her mind did not work that way. She preferred not to dwell on how it might work, not to speculate. Although the encounter had been an upsetting one, almost as disturbing as seeing that woman slumped on the Underground platform, on that morning which seemed so long ago now.

When she got home, Letty found Mrs Pope standing in the hall with a leaflet in her hand.

'Help the Aged,' she declared. 'Good, serviceable clothing is needed for the aged overseas.'

Letty could think of nothing to say.

After they had parted from the women, Norman turned to Edwin. 'You must let me know the damage and I'll settle with you.'

'Oh, that's all right. I used mostly luncheon vouchers – the extra hardly amounted to anything – you must let me do this,' said Edwin quickly, for he was sometimes haunted by a picture of Norman in his bedsitter while he himself occupied a whole house.

'Well, thanks, chum,' said Norman awkwardly. 'It wasn't so bad, really, was it.'

'No, it passed off quite well – better than I expected in some ways, but I don't like the look of Marcia.'

'You're telling me! I should say she was going right round the bend. Still, she is under the doctor, that's something. And that social worker goes to see her.'

'Yes, rather too often, she said. People do seem to be keeping an eye on her.'

With this they left the subject, but Edwin did say something to the effect that they must do it again some time, repeat the lunch invitation to Letty and Marcia. But it was a comfort to feel that this need not be for some time to come and that for the moment they had done their duty.

Sixteen

ALTHOUGH HE HAD been dead for some years, Marcia still missed the old cat, Snowy, and one evening she found herself particularly reminded of him when she came across one of his dishes in the cupboard under the sink. She was surprised and a little upset to notice that it still had some dried-up fragments of Kit-e-Kat adhering to it. Had she then not washed it up after his death? It would seem not. This might not have surprised an observer, but Marcia regarded herself as a meticulous housekeeper and she had always been especially careful with Snowy's dishes, keeping them, in her own words, 'spotlessly clean'.

The finding of the dish gave her a desire to visit the cat's grave which was somewhere at the bottom of the garden. When Snowy had died, Mr Smith, who had lived next door before Nigel and Priscilla came, had dug a grave and Marcia had laid Snowy in it, his body wrapped in a piece of her old blue ripple-cloth dressing gown which he used to sleep on. In the midst of life we are in death, she had thought, feeling the significance of the cloth and its associations. She had not marked the grave in any way, but she remembered where it was, for when she walked down the path she would think, Snowy's grave; but as time went on she forgot the exact spot and now, in the season of high summer with the weeds flourishing, she could not find it at all. That part of the garden was so overgrown that she could hardly tell where the path and flowerbed met. There was a sprawling bush of catmint, so the grave must be somewhere near there because Snowy had loved to roll in the plant, but it was quite indiscernible now, though Marcia parted the covering of leaves and weeds with her hands. Then it occurred to her that if she were to dig in that bit of the garden, she would surely come upon the grave, perhaps uncover a fragment of the blue ripple-cloth and then even find the bones.

She went to the shed and fetched a spade, but it was very heavy and if she had ever wielded it in the past, she was certainly unable to now. After my operation of course, she thought, trying once more to move the earth and the thick clotting of weeds – dandelions, thistles and bindweed, plants with strong matted roots.

It was thus that Priscilla saw her, crouched at the bottom of the garden. What was she *doing,* trying to dig with that heavy spade? It was worrying and upsetting, for the old – especially Miss Ivory – were perpetually nagging at her conscience. Not only was she a neighbour but also what Janice Brabner called 'disadvantaged' and that, whatever it might mean – Priscilla wasn't absolutely sure – was certainly something to worry about. Of course, Nigel had asked Miss Ivory if she wanted her lawn cut but she had preferred it the way it was and one couldn't bully the elderly, their independence was their last remaining treasure and must be respected. All the same, one could perhaps offer a little gardening assistance, digging, for example . . . but not *now,* when Priscilla had people coming to dinner, the avocados to prepare and mayonnaise to make. Perhaps it was a fine enough evening to have drinks outside on the little patio they had made, but the view of the neglected garden next door would detract from the elegance of the occasion, and if Miss Ivory was going to go on digging in this disturbing way something would have to be done about it. But now, to Priscilla's relief, she was going back towards the house, dragging the heavy spade behind her. One had to cling to the hope that she knew what she was doing.

Back in the kitchen, Marcia couldn't remember what she had gone out for, then the sight of the cat's dish soaking in the sink reminded her. There had been no trace of the grave and she was not strong enough to go on digging for it. She supposed she should have something to eat, but it was a bother to cook anything and she didn't want to disturb her supply of tins. So she just made a cup of tea and put plenty of sugar in it, like the tea at the hospital. 'Cup of tea, Miss Ivory? Sugar, dear?' It gave Marcia a warm feeling to remember those days and that nice woman – Nancy, they called her – coming round with the tea.

On that same summer evening Letty was helping Mrs Pope and little furry Mrs Musson to sort out clothes that had been sent in response to the appeal for aged refugees.

'What would you think if somebody gave you this?' said Mrs Pope, holding up a bright red mini-skirt. 'People have no idea of what is needed.'

'Some oriental women are very small,' said Letty doubtfully. 'So I suppose they could wear it. Of course one doesn't really know what they need – it's so difficult to visualize . . .' The horror of the pictures on Mrs Pope's television screen seemed so totally unconnected with the heaps of unsuitable garments piled on the floor of Mrs Musson's dining room. Mrs Pope had refused to receive the clothes in her own house. 'Nobody would expect a woman in her eighties . . .' she maintained, and of course she had a point there, even if it was not absolutely clear what it was. Letty suspected that it might be an old deep-rooted fear of 'fevers and diseases' that made her avoid too close contact with other people's cast-off clothes. As for nobody expecting a woman in her eighties to house this jumble of old garments, that really had nothing to do with it, for Mrs Pope did exactly those things that she wanted to do which made Letty realize that perhaps getting older had some advantages, few though these might be.

During the months since her retirement, Letty had tried conscientiously to enter into the life around her in the north-west London suburb where she now found herself. This meant, as Edwin had imagined her, taking part in the activities of the church, sitting rather far back, trying to discover what church-going held for people, apart from habit and convention, wondering if it would hold anything for her and if so what form this would take. On a bitter cold evening in March she joined a little group, hardly more than the two or three gathered together, shuffling round the Stations of the Cross. It was the third Wednesday in Lent and there had been snow, now hard and frozen on the ground. The church was icy. The knees of elderly women bent creakily at each Station, hands had to grasp the edge of a pew to pull the body up again. 'From pain to pain, from woe to woe . . .' they recited, but Letty's thoughts had been on herself and how she should arrange the rest of her life. Easter was of course better, with daffodils in the church and people making an effort with their clothes, but Whitsun was bitterly cold, with a leaden grey sky and the church heating turned off. Did people then only go for the light and warmth, the coffee after the Sunday morning service and a friendly word from the vicar?

Once Edwin had come to the service and Letty had greeted him so warmly that he must have taken fright, for he had not appeared again. 'Oh, he goes round to a lot of churches, as it takes his fancy,' somebody had pointed out and of course Letty knew that this was true. Not even Father G. had his undivided allegiance. 'He's a widower,' Mrs Pope had said, 'but of course you know that, working with him. And he took a lot of trouble finding a room for you when that black man bought the house you were living in. He must think a lot of you – he spoke very warmly.' For Mrs Pope this was going far, but the doubtful prospect of Edwin's 'warmth' did nothing to warm Letty's cold heart.

Now at least she felt that she was doing something useful, helping to sort out and pack clothes for aged refugees. She would have preferred something a little nearer home, people she could have pictured actually wearing the clothes, even the scarlet miniskirt, but it was not to be. Everything at all suitable was just bundled into black plastic bags, while the less suitable was cast aside for jumble.

'You'll be giving the room a good clean out after this, of course,' said Mrs Pope and Mrs Musson had to agree, feeling bound to point out that she cleaned the room every day anyway.

'I suppose the clothes could have been sent to the church hall?' Letty suggested.

'Oh, that wouldn't have done at all,' said Mrs Pope, but Letty, even with her newly acquired experience of parish affairs, did not yet possess the particular item of esoteric knowledge that would enable her to solve this problem. All was never as it might seem to be.

'What a lovely evening,' Letty said, looking out of the window. 'All that laburnum!'

Norman, coming back from work, did not notice the laburnums in full flower in the square garden, but his heart lifted when he saw that an old car, which had been dumped there for over a week, appeared to have been removed. He had got on to the police and the council about that, and the fine summer evening gave him a sense of achievement, an unusual and agreeable sensation for him. This gave way to a feeling of restlessness, so that after he had fried bacon and tomatoes and opened a small tin of his favourite butter beans, it did not seem quite enough to settle down in his bedsitter with the *Evening Standard* and the radio. He felt he wanted to go out, take a bus somewhere to another part of London, any bus, the first one that came, if one ever *did* come, he added sardonically.

A bus did come and he got on it and took a ticket to Clapham Common, realizing after he had done so that Edwin lived in that direction, but of course it was most unlikely that he would run into him. He was probably at some fancy service at one of his many churches.

On top of the bus, Norman settled down for the long ride – it cost enough anyway, he thought. He sat on the front seat, like a visitor to London, observing the scene around him, sights passing before his eyes – well-known landmarks, buildings, the river; then gardens and people in them doing things to lawns and hedges, and in the roads men engaged in the rituals concerned with the motor car. When he got to a suitable stopping place he climbed down from the bus and began to walk aimlessly. Now he was not at all sure why he had come or what he was going to do when he got there, wherever 'there' might be. Turning off the common he came to a side road, and just as Edwin had done some time ago he realized that he was looking at the name of the road where Marcia lived. But unlike Edwin he did not turn away but began to walk down it, though with no clear plan in his mind. He certainly did not intend to call on her, he didn't even remember the number of her house. But wouldn't it be easy to pick it out, he asked himself, wouldn't it stand out as being different from the smartly tarted-up suburban semi-detached Victorian villas with their pastel-coloured front doors, carriage lamps, paved patios and car-ports?

Of course he was right. Marcia's house, with its flaking green and cream paint, dusty laurels and dingy curtains, was unmistakable. He stood on the opposite side of the road and gazed in stunned fascination, very much as he had gazed at the mummified animals in the British Museum. The house looked deserted, the curtains half drawn, and although it was a warm evening there was no crack of window open. The garden, as far as Norman could see, was totally neglected, but a magnificent old laburnum tree was in full flower. Its branches drooped over a ramshackle little garden shed, and as he stood there he saw Marcia coming out of the shed with her arms full of milk bottles. Her hair was quite white and she was wearing an old cotton dress patterned with large pink flowers. It was such a strange sight that he was as if rooted to the spot. He had a feeling that she had seen him and for an instant they seemed to stand staring at each other – again it was like the British Museum encounter with the mummified animals – giving no sign of mutual recognition. Then Marcia disappeared from view, presumably going into the back of her house, he thought.

Norman crossed the road with no clear idea of what he should do. Ought he to go up to the door and ring the bell, make himself known? His instinct was to run away, but before he could make up his mind he saw that a young woman was approaching the house from the opposite direction. She walked purposefully and when she saw Norman, loitering in front of Marcia's house, she said sharply, 'Going to see somebody here, are you?'

'Oh no, just taking a walk,' said Norman quickly.

'I've been watching you,' Janice went on. 'Do you know somebody in this house?'

'What's that got to do with you?' Norman snapped.

'We have to be on the lookout – everybody has to. There've been some break-ins round here lately.'

'Charming, I must say!' Norman burst out. 'I shouldn't think Marcia Ivory's got much worth stealing.'

'You know her then? I'm sorry, but you know how it is – one gets so suspicious.' Janice smiled. 'As a matter of fact I was just going to call on Miss Ivory – I'm a volunteer social worker.'

'Keeping an eye on her, are you?'

'That's it. I pop in every now and then.'

'That's good. Well, cheerio, I must be on my way.' Norman began to move off.

'Aren't you going in to see her now you're here?' Janice asked.

'Oh, I have seen her,' said Norman, some distance away by now. And of course, in a sense, that was true. That sight of her with the milk bottles surely counted as seeing and it had been enough. Once seen never forgotten, he thought. But at least he would be able to tell Edwin that although Marcia's house looked a bit grotty, as the modern expression had it, a brisk young social worker was keeping an eye on her. It didn't necessarily follow, though, that he would tell Edwin about this evening – he didn't want to have to explain what he had been doing in that part of London, what sudden impulse had sent him there. It had been just one of those things and Edwin probably wouldn't understand that.

In the house Janice was saying in her brightest tone, 'I see you had a visitor just now.'

Marcia stared in the disconcerting way she always met any comment or question.

'The gentleman I saw in the road.'

'Oh, *him!*' Marcia was scornful. 'That was just somebody I used to work with. I don't want anybody like *that* coming to see me.'

Janice sighed. Better leave the subject of the gentleman visitor, that funny little man. 'And how have you been getting on?' she asked. 'Been shopping today, have you?'

Seventeen

WALKING IN THE wood Letty came upon a sheet of wild garlic. 'Oh, how lovely!' she exclaimed.

'You should have seen the bluebells,' Marjorie said, with the enthusiastically proprietary air of the country dweller. 'They were wonderful this year, but they're nearly over now. You should have come a fortnight ago when they were at their best.'

You didn't ask me then, Letty thought, for it was only now, when David was away on a visit to his mother (in her ninetieth year, Letty recalled), that Marjorie had suggested that she might like a few days in the country.

'This is almost like old times, isn't it?' Marjorie went on.

'Yes, in a way,' Letty agreed, taking note of the 'almost', 'but so much has happened.'

'Yes, hasn't it! Who would ever have thought ... that first time I met David, I really had no idea ...' Marjorie proceeded to recall that first meeting and the subsequent development of her relationship with the man she was about to marry. Letty allowed her to ramble on while she looked around the wood, remembering its autumn carpet of beech leaves and wondering if it could be the kind of place to lie down in and prepare for death when life became too much to be endured. Had an old person – a pensioner, of course – ever been found in such a situation? No doubt it would be difficult to lie undiscovered for long, for this wood was a favourite walking place for bustling women with dogs. It was not the kind of fancy she could indulge with Marjorie or even dwell on too much herself. Danger lay in that direction.

Marjorie still had the idea that Letty might find a room at Holmhurst and that evening they were to have supper with Miss Doughty, the resident warden.

Beth Doughty was a smartly dressed woman in her middle forties, with a rigidly controlled hairstyle, sharp eyes, and heavy make-up which gave her a curiously old-fashioned look. She poured generous tots of gin, explaining that in her job you really needed what she rather oddly described as 'moral support'. Letty found herself wondering if she really liked old people, but perhaps efficiency was more important than liking and she certainly gave the impression of being highly capable.

'Do you think Letty could find a place at Holmhurst?' Marjorie asked. 'You thought there might be another vacancy soon.'

'You wouldn't like living here, not after living in London,' Beth declared. 'Just look at them now – come to the window.'

Letty stood looking out, glass in hand. Three old ladies – an uncomfortable number, hinting at awkwardness – were walking slowly round the garden. There was nothing particularly remarkable about them except their remoteness from any kind of life. Suddenly Letty felt indignant with Marjorie for supposing that she would be content with this sort of existence when she herself was going to marry a handsome clergyman. It was all of a piece with that life of forty years ago, when Letty had always trailed behind her friend, but there was no need to follow the same pattern now. As Beth Doughty topped up her glass, she resolved that a room in Holmhurst was the last thing she'd come to – better to lie down in the wood under the beech leaves and bracken and wait quietly for death.

'This is one of Father Lydell's favourite dishes,' said Beth, bringing a covered casserole to the table. '*Poulet niçoise* – I hope you like it.'

'Oh, yes,' Letty murmured, remembering the times she had eaten *poulet niçoise* at Marjorie's house. Had David Lydell gone all round the village sampling the cooking of the unattached women before deciding which one to settle with? Certainly the dish they were eating this evening was well up to standard.

Afterwards Marjorie said, 'It was rather funny about the *poulet niçoise* and the way Beth had to let us know that she had asked David in to meals – she made a dead set at him, you know.'

'And that wine we had – Orvieto, wasn't it?'

'Yes – another of David's favourites. It's really quite amusing, isn't it?'

Letty was doubtful about this, for the ridiculous little episode had given her a glimpse of something deeper that she did not particularly want to probe.

'I do wonder how Beth Doughty manages to rise to all that gin,' Marjorie went on, 'so expensive now. Luckily David doesn't care for spirits.'

'Well, that's a blessing, isn't it,' Letty agreed, feeling that there was something obscurely wrong about this juxtaposition of spirits with blessing, but unable to supply an appropriate modification.

That evening Marcia paid a visit to the doctor. She had not made an appointment and was not even sure which of the three doctors she would be seeing, but it did not really matter since none of them was Mr Strong. She was content to sit for anything up to two hours, not even glancing through the tattered magazines but just observing the other people waiting. Most of these, in her opinion, need not have been there at all. She wondered how many of them, if any, had undergone 'major surgery', as she had. The majority were young, as if they had just come from work, and appeared to have nothing whatever the matter with them. All they wanted was a certificate. Wasting the doctor's time, she thought – no wonder the National Health Service was in such financial trouble.

When her name was called she was still indignant, and had it been the young woman doctor or the honey-voiced Middle-Eastern one behind the desk she would have gone on seething. It was neither of these but the one she called her 'own' doctor, a middle-aged man with a kindly, anxious expression. This was the doctor who had sent her into hospital in the first place, who had seen that lump on her breast.

'Well, Miss Ivory...' his hands moved among a sheaf of papers. 'And how's the world treating you?' Mastectomy, he thought. Odd, difficult; a glib but accurate diagnosis of this particular patient. 'How have you been?'

Marcia needed no more encouragement but proceeded to tell him. What she said was not altogether coherent or even relevant, but the doctor was given a decided impression that all was not quite as it should be. She grumbled about the social worker, her neighbours who wanted to mow her lawn, her inability to locate the grave of her dead cat and the suspicion that 'somebody' might have moved it, the difficulty of keeping a check on her collection of milk bottles, a man she used to work with who had come spying on her, the closing of a branch of Sainsbury's near her old office – it was all jumbled up in a great flood of complaint. The doctor was used to patients going on in this way, so he only half listened while examining her and taking her blood pressure and wondering what on earth to do with her. She told him that she was due for another check-up at the hospital soon, so that rather took things out of his hands. No doubt Strong's boys would suggest something. In the meantime he urged her to look after herself and to get more to eat – she was much too thin.

'Oh, I've never been a big eater,' Marcia declared with her usual pride. 'But nobody can say that I don't keep a good table. You should just see my store cupboard.'

'I'm sure you're an admirable housekeeper,' said the doctor diplomatically, 'but you must promise me that you'll go home and cook yourself a really good meal. Not just a cup of tea and a bit of bread and butter, Miss Ivory. I don't know what Mr Strong is going to say when he sees you looking so thin.'

The mention of Mr Strong's name had the desired effect and Marcia assured the doctor that she would go back at once and cook something. All the way home she thought of Mr Strong and the kind of meal the surgeon would most likely be having this evening – steak, perhaps, or a nice bit of fish, salmon or halibut, with fresh vegetables from his garden. She was sure there were vegetables in that garden although she had not been able to see the back of it when she had gone to look at his house last year. It might be possible to catch a glimpse of beans and lettuces or cabbages and broccoli – Marcia's gardening days were so long past that she had no clear recollection of what vegetables would be in season. Should she go there now on a bus and make sure? Perhaps there was a side entrance to the house which would give her a view of the back garden...

It was beginning to get dark and while she hesitated a bus drew up at the stop, illuminated like some noble galleon waiting to take her on a voyage of discovery. Inside the brilliantly lit interior, women who had come from late-night Thursday shopping in the West End chatted and compared the things they had bought – wasting their money, Marcia thought, choosing an empty seat in the front and holding herself aloof from the chattering women.

When she got to the stop for Mr Strong's house, she realized that even if she could see the vegetable garden it was now too dark to discern what was growing there, and anyway she had forgetten why she had wanted to see them in the first place. And perhaps there wasn't a vegetable garden, just a lawn with a herbaceous border or even a tennis court. But it didn't matter, she thought, as she approached the house, for now she saw that it, like the bus, was brilliantly lit up – resembling a great liner in mid-ocean rather than a galleon, what she imagined the *Queen Mary* might have been – and that elegantly dressed people were alighting from cars and walking up the drive. The Strongs were obviously giving a party.

Marcia stationed herself on the pavement opposite, instinctively choosing a dark corner under a tree, away from the street lamp. Was it a dinner party or an evening party? She did not feel capable of guessing what kind of an evening party, for she could only think of 'wine and cheese', which seemed altogether unworthy of Mr Strong.

When she had been in hospital, there had naturally been talk in the ward about the various consultants when they came on their rounds, and speculation as to their wives and families. Some of them, of course, had married other doctors or nurses, women they had met in the course of their work, but it was always said that Mr Strong had done rather better than that. It was rumoured that he had married the daughter of a 'diplomat' who had a house in Belgrave Square. Marcia had never quite believed this, not wishing to speculate overmuch on Mr Strong's wife anyway, but now, watching the guests arrive, she was prepared to believe that there might be something in it. In a kind of dream, she stood watching until there was a gap in the cars arriving and it seemed that no more would come.

Then suddenly she found herself thinking about Norman and the way she had seen him standing on the pavement opposite her house when she was putting milk bottles into her shed. She had resented his being there, resented what seemed his prying curiosity into her affairs. Could it be that her standing outside Mr Strong's house would be seen in the same way?

She looked up at the house and then crossed the road, so that she could hear voices and laughter coming from a room on the ground floor. Then she moved slowly on, making her way back to the bus stop. As luck would have it, the right number bus was just coming up to the stop and she had to run to catch it.

The exertion was almost too much for her and she collapsed on to the nearest seat, unable to collect her wits for a moment to ask for her ticket. But after a while she recovered, partly out of self-defence and resentment at the loud patronizing voice of the conductress's 'All right, dear?'

'Of course I'm all right,' she said stiffly.

But when she got home she realized that going to the doctor and then on to Mr Strong's house had made her more tired than usual. Well, it would stand to reason ... she found herself thinking of the kind of thing Norman said. And 'it takes it out of you' – that was another of his expressions.

Sitting down at the kitchen table, she remembered that she had promised the doctor that she would go home and get herself a good meal but the thought of having to cook was too much for her. Elderly people didn't need much food, anyway – surely the doctor must realize that? A cup of tea, of course; that was a stimulant, and now that she had discovered tea bags it was so much less trouble. At the supermarket she had bought a packet of 144 tea bags which she reckoned ought to last her about seven weeks all but one day. But long before that she would be at the hospital; the card indicating the date of her appointment at Mr Strong's out-patients' clinic was on the mantelpiece. Not that she needed reminding, especially not after what she had just seen.

The thought of it impelled her to go to the store cupboard to fetch a suitable tin of something. There was still a tin of pilchards left over from Snowy's larder, but perhaps luncheon meat would be better? It had a little key to open it, but before she had gone very far the metal tab broke off and she lacked the strength to manoeuvre it any further. So she abandoned the half-opened tin on the draining board and contented herself with a couple of digestive biscuits, which was really all she wanted.

'You didn't go in then, or make yourself known?' Edwin asked Norman.

'What do you take me for! Can you imagine the sort of reception I'd have got! She was standing by the shed with a pile of milk bottles in her arms and she must have seen me.'

'Yes, and knowing what she's like I can imagine you wouldn't want to intrude,' Edwin agreed.

'Intrude!' Norman gave his bitter little laugh. 'That's a nice way of putting it. I met that social worker and she thought I was casing the joint.'

'Well, she's right to be careful – there's always a risk of that these days,' Edwin said. 'I'll stroll past there one evening and see if there's anything I can do.'

But of course Edwin was not at all sure what there would be, if anything. The idea of being able to 'do' something for Marcia was so improbable that he had only said it to ease his conscience a little. After all, he and Norman had worked with her and it would no doubt seem to an outsider that they might be just the people to be in a position to help her or at least to offer help, to show willing, as Norman might say. This particular evening, being Corpus Christi, Edwin had a service at his own church, with an open-air procession, which started at eight o'clock and would probably last for at least an hour. After that he would go to the pub with Father G. so there wouldn't really be time to visit Marcia. Perhaps the weekend would be better, Saturday afternoon or Sunday before Evensong. Then he wouldn't have to stay too long.

'Of course, I'm not often down that way,' Norman pointed out. 'Not exactly my stamping ground, Clapham.'

'You're really nearer to Letty,' Edwin said.

'So what? You're surely not suggesting I should drop in on her?'

For some reason the idea of this caused the two men to break into laughter, so that what had started out as a serious attempt to deal with a social problem turned into a kind of joke. But there was no reason why, as Norman put it, they should fall about laughing at the prospect. It wasn't all that funny. Nervous reaction, perhaps, but why nervous, Norman wondered. Something in the subconscious, Edwin suggested, but that set them off into more laughter, the idea of Letty and Marcia being somehow mixed up in their subconsciousnesses. It was not an area they were in the habit of discussing or even thinking about.

Eighteen

'MISS IVORY, AREN'T you going to let me in?'

As she stood on the doorstep, Janice wondered whether anyone else had been to see Marcia during her fortnight in Greece. This seemed unlikely because it wasn't as if Marcia was an invalid or unable to cope, even if she was a bit eccentric. And anyway she was Janice's special pigeon, if you could put it like that.

There was a fine display of late summer flowers in the gardens along the road – dahlias and asters, early chrysanthemums and a second flowering of roses, and even Marcia's garden had some tall yellow daisies clustering round what Nigel and Priscilla called the milk-bottle shed. They had never been inside it but had often seen Marcia going in and out with the bottles. It seemed a curiously dotty occupation, but harmless enough – just the kind of thing Marcia would spend her time doing, but no more to be condemned than other people's preoccupation with collecting matchboxes or cigarette cards. One *must* respect people as individuals – her acquaintance with Marcia had taught Janice that, if nothing else. All the same, she felt that she really must try to persuade Marcia to take a holiday. Not Greece, of course, or indeed anywhere 'abroad' – one could hardly imagine Marcia in a taverna, eating octopus or anything that wasn't meat and two veg – but a few days in Bournemouth or a coach tour of the Cotswolds would be just the thing to set her up for the winter.

'Miss Ivory!' Janice rang the bell again and banged on the door. It was most unlikely that she was out, though perhaps it was just possible. Should she try the door to see if it was open? Janice did try it and it was locked. Perhaps if she went round to the back she would be able to get into the house, though if Marcia had gone out she would surely have locked the back door as well. If only Nigel and Priscilla were here she could ask them, but Janice knew that they were in Sardinia, lying on some beach, not even thinking of their fashionable little house in that up-and-coming district by the common and their peculiar next-door neighbour. One certainly got completely away from that kind of thing on holiday, Janice thought, not without bitterness.

It was then that she noticed several bottles of milk, not on the front step but in a little wooden container round the side, no doubt an arrangement made for milk to be left when Marcia went out to work, to keep it out of the sun or safe from thieves. This sight alarmed her, and she hurried round to the back door – perhaps Marcia was lying ill in bed, unable even to get downstairs to take in her milk. If she could get into the back of the house she could call to her, and if she was in bed Marcia would answer. Or she might have had a fall and be unable to move or get to the telephone. Did Marcia have a telephone? Probably not. With neighbours away she could lie for hours, helpless ... Janice knew in theory every kind of situation that could arise, but when she peered through the glass panel of the back door she was not prepared for the sight of Marcia sitting at the table, slumped into unconsciousness, possibly even death.

Janice noticed the cup of tea and the tin of biscuits ('Family Assorted') on the table, as she knocked feebly on the door, calling

'Miss Ivory' in a half-fearful tone, hardly expecting or wishing for an answer. Then she tried the handle of the door. It opened and she realized that it was perfectly possible for her to go in.

'Of course she's not in my parish,' said Father G., with a hint of impatience. 'You know what these parish boundaries are – one road's in, the next one isn't.'

'I know that,' said Edwin. 'I was just going to stroll along that way and I thought you might like to come too – after all, it's a nice evening for a walk. She's a funny sort of woman, as I told you, we may not even be invited in.'

'Who is my neighbour?' Father G. mused, as he and Edwin came to the road where Marcia lived. 'Surely one has preached often enough on that text? Perhaps that's where we go wrong – obviously it *is* – when my reaction to your suggestion is that the person in question isn't in my parish.'

'Well, she must be in somebody's parish,' Edwin pointed out.

'She certainly is,' said Father G. promptly, and he named a well-known local vicar, 'but I don't think he goes in much for parochial visiting. Trendy Tony,' he added, unable to resist the uncharitable comment. 'Rock-and-roll and extempore prayers.'

'Of course there's a social worker who goes to see her regularly, keeps an eye on her, as the saying is, but when I saw her earlier in the year – we all had lunch together, you see – I thought perhaps I ought to do something about her, make more of an effort.'

'What about this other woman you were telling me about, there was another who worked with you, wasn't there? I should have thought . . .' Father G. suggested, with the comfortable assumption of so much that could be left to the women.

'Yes, in a way you would have thought . . .' Edwin smiled. 'But then you don't know Marcia – Miss Ivory. Come to that, who does know her?'

'Who does know anyone?' said Father G., hardly contributing to the solution of the problem of Marcia.

'Well, this is it, I believe – the house where she lives. You can see how different it looks from the others and that tells its own story.'

Father G. was used to visiting shabby houses, but he had to admit the contrast between Marcia's and the other houses in the road. 'You'd better go up to the door,' he said. 'You know her, and if she's a difficult woman the sight of me might put her off. She might refuse to open the door.'

Janice, coming round the side of the house, was encouraged rather than put off by the sight of Father G., in his priestly cloak, standing behind Edwin. Although she had little use for the Church of England, or indeed for any organized religion apart from a mild, superstitious veneration for what she thought of as 'Catholics', she could not deny that it sometimes had its uses. The fact that this respectable-looking stranger – for so Edwin appeared to her – was accompanied by a clergyman was reassuring. They would certainly know what was the best thing to do.

'If you've come to see Miss Ivory,' she said, 'I'm afraid something's happened. She seems to be ill, or . . .' She did not like to say 'dead'. 'She's sitting at the table in her kitchen, not moving – I saw through the window. I was just going to find help . . .'

As it happened, Janice could not have met at this moment with two persons better able to assist her. Edwin had come home one evening some years ago to find his wife Phyllis unconscious in the kitchen, about to put a shepherd's pie in the oven; Father G. was often obliged to enter houses where people were on the point of death or had already died; indeed he preferred this type of situation to normal parish visiting, with its awkward conversation and the inevitable cups of tea and sweet biscuits. Both the men were prepared to take control.

The main thing was that Marcia was not *dead.* She even smiled faintly at Janice who was fussing about packing a case of suitable things for hospital while they waited for the ambulance.

'It was amazing,' Janice said afterwards. 'When I came to look out her things, there was a drawer full of new Marks and Sparks nighties – not at all what you'd imagine Miss Ivory wearing, judging by the rest of her clothes. All brand new and never worn – she must have been saving them up for something.'

After the ambulance had gone, with Marcia and Janice in it, the two men were left alone in the house. They had all been sitting in the kitchen where Janice had made tea. Edwin felt awkward, now that Marcia had been removed, as if he had no right to be sitting in her house when he had never been in it before.

'It's a strange relationship, working with women like that,' he said. 'The curious intimacy of the office is very definitely *not* repeated outside it – one would not presume . . .' He remembered how he and Norman had been overcome with laughter at the idea of Norman visiting Letty or of any kind of social contact between the four of them. Visiting Marcia had always seemed an awesome prospect, hardly even to be contemplated.

'You never thought of coming to see her, living as near as you do, just a few steps across the common?' Father G.'s tone was enquiring rather than reproachful.

'I thought of it – once or twice I came near to it – but I never did.'

Father G. finished his tea and stood up, holding the cup in his hand. 'Do you think we should . . .?'

'Wash up? Oh, I think Mrs Brabner, the social worker, will probably see to that. I don't think we should get involved.'

So the men left the house, remembering to lock up behind them. Neither had commented on the state of the kitchen and hall, the dust and other evidences of long neglect. Father G. genuinely did not notice such things and Edwin, with a general impression that all was not quite as it should be, still preserved the same detachment towards this as towards other aspects of Marcia's life. What he did carry away with him was an irrelevant detail, the sight of a half-opened tin of luncheon meat still on the draining board. It had always surprised him how ineffectual women were when it came to opening a perfectly simple tin.

It was natural for them both to feel the need of a strengthening and reviving drink when they found themselves some distance away from Marcia's house. They had undergone an unexpectedly upsetting experience. Little had Edwin imagined that a casual stroll across the common in the direction of Marcia's house could have such an outcome. Yet what had the outcome been? Marcia had been found in a distressed condition, but she had been taken away in an ambulance to hospital where she would receive the best possible care. There was nothing further that anyone could do. All the same, the need for a drink was uppermost in his mind, and then supper – the events of the last hour had delayed the evening meal and it was well known that an upsetting experience had unexpected results, not necessarily the most suitable or desirable ones. There was a hollow feeling in his stomach and he remembered that he had not eaten since lunch.

'You'll stay and take pot luck with me?' he said to Father G., knowing that there would be little cheer at the vicarage. He at least had the remains of a casserole in the larder.

'That's good of you – I'm quite hungry.'

Edwin poured sherry. Had it been the kind of upsetting experience that called for brandy? he wondered. On the whole he thought not, for it did not touch him personally. All the same, he ought to get in touch with Letty, who would no doubt want to visit Marcia in hospital. Come to that, he supposed they all ought to; the three of them should cluster round her bed. Again he found himself wanting to smile, almost to laugh, and if Norman had been with him at that moment instead of Father G. he felt that the smile might have turned most regrettably into laughter. It was disconcerting the way this happened – any idea of the women now seemed to be a subject for comedy. But with Father G. it was different. In the midst of life he was so continually in death . . .

'Do you think I should visit her in hospital?' Father G. was asking. 'I easily could – the chaplain there is an old friend. She might feel that as I saw her, found her, as it were . . .'

'I don't know what Marcia would feel. But I'm sure she would like to have a visit,' said Edwin uncertainly, for he was not at all sure. How could anyone be sure about Marcia?

The next morning Edwin had to break the news to Norman.

'I should've thought a loony bin would have been more to the point than hospital,' said Norman, in a rough way that might have concealed an obscure emotion. 'What are we expected to do – send flowers by Interflora – have a whip round in the office?' He was standing by the window and shook himself like an angry little dog coming out of the water.

'I'll get some flowers and take them round – the hospital's not far from where I live,' said Edwin soothingly. 'And I'll get in touch with Letty.'

Norman fumbled in his trousers pocket and produced a fifty-pence piece. 'You'd better say they're from all of us, the flowers. Here's something towards it.'

'Thank you. I won't ask to see her, just leave the flowers,' Edwin said. It was a relief that the general embarrassment of the situation had not made them burst out laughing, as he had feared. Perhaps there were some things, hospitals especially, that were still sacred.

'I wouldn't want to go and see her,' Norman said. 'I did go

when my brother-in-law, Ken, was in hospital, but then he had nobody and being the blood-tie and that I felt I had to.'

Edwin was about to point out that a brother-in-law wasn't exactly a blood relation but he thought it best to leave the subject, and if they got to talking about people having nobody it might well be remembered that Marcia also came into that category.

In Mrs Pope's house the telephone rang just as she and Letty were settling down to watch television. They quite often did this now, and although it had started by Mrs Pope suggesting that Letty might like to watch the news or some improving programme of cultural or scientific interest, there was now hardly an evening when Letty did not come down to watch whatever happened to be on the box, whether it was worthy of attention or not.

'Oh, bother, who can that be?' said Mrs Pope, going out into the hall. 'It's for you,' she said accusingly to Letty. 'People ought not to ring up at such a time.'

Letty went apologetically to the telephone. Of course there was really no suitable time to ring people in the evening now that television had been invented, for with the choice of three programmes one of them was certain to be the one somebody was watching. Even the worst had their adherents and who was to judge what was 'worst', the kind of thing that nobody could possibly want to see?

When Letty came back into the room, Mrs Pope looked up expectantly. Letty did not have many telephone calls and never seemed to make any. 'It was a man's voice,' she said encouragingly, 'so I knew it couldn't be your friend in the country.'

'No, it was Edwin Braithwaite.'

'Oh, Mr Braithwaite.' Mrs Pope waited for Letty to go on.

'He was ringing to tell me that Marcia Ivory who used to work in the office had been taken into hospital.'

'Taken into hospital!' Mrs Pope's interest was immediately

aroused and Letty had to repeat what Edwin had told her about Marcia's collapse and the summoning of the ambulance. This led on to further probing from Mrs Pope so that in the end Letty found herself having to recount the history of Marcia's operation and to supply as many details as she knew.

'But how did Mr Braithwaite know about it?' Mrs Pope asked.

'Apparently he found her, discovered her in a state of collapse in her kitchen.'

'That doesn't sound like him,' Mrs Pope objected.

'I think he had a clergyman with him – would it be the vicar, perhaps, paying a call?'

'Yes, I suppose it could be that. But don't you think it more likely that he and the lady were friends, after all, working together and living so near . . .'

Letty found herself unable to comment on this supposition. A relationship between Edwin and Marcia was really going too far. You ought to see her, she thought of saying, but a charitable impulse held her back. One did not make remarks of that kind about a person lying dangerously ill in hospital. And life was in many ways so fantastic that for all Letty knew there might indeed be something between Edwin and Marcia. A married woman – and she must not forget that Mrs Pope was that – might very well be able to detect subtle shades of meaning in a relationship which would be lost on the inexperienced Letty. For of course there had been Mr Pope, no more to Letty than a photograph in Mrs Pope's sitting room, and it was not for her to probe beyond that patient-looking face in the silver frame. And now the television screen was beginning to claim their full attention.

By a coincidence they were taken into a hospital setting, not in a popular romantic way but as the background for surgical investigation. An operation was in progress, with commentary and informative pictures.

'Amazing what they can do now,' said Mrs Pope, in a satisfied tone. 'But of course your friend won't be having anything like this.'

'Oh, no . . .' Letty was apologetic. 'I expect she'll just be lying there.'

'If we had colour,' Mrs Pope went on, 'we should be able to see *exactly* what the surgeon was doing. There would be *real* blood, not tomato ketchup, as I've heard they use in these violent films.'

'I don't think I should want to see exactly,' said Letty, turning away from the black and white close-up of a pulsating heart and concentrating on her tapestry.

'We have to see these things, whether we like it or not,' Mrs Pope declared, for she had noticed Letty turning away from the screen. 'No point in shutting your eyes to them.'

Letty wanted to protest – they could just as easily have been watching a Western on the other channel, but they didn't *have* to watch that either.

'Has Mr Braithwaite got colour?' Mrs Pope asked.

Letty had to admit that she didn't know, or even whether Edwin had television at all. He had never mentioned it, in the same way that he had never given any indication of having any special feeling for Marcia. If anyone had that, it was Norman, she felt, thoroughly confused.

Nineteen

MARCIA HAD ALWAYS appreciated the drama of an ambulance and even wanted to ride in one, but when the time came she was hardly in a position to realize that she was at last achieving this unusual ambition.

'Unreachable inside a room' she may have been, yet there was no sense of that little room becoming an everywhere, in the fantasy of an earlier poet. No fragment of poetry from long ago lingered in Marcia's mind as she lay under a red blanket. She had been aware of people coming into the house as she sat at the kitchen table, thinking she heard Edwin's voice and imagining herself back in the office, but where was Norman? She was also half conscious of Janice Brabner fussing around her, seeming to panic a bit. Marcia tried to tell her that she had half a dozen new nighties, never worn, tucked away in a drawer upstairs, and also to explain about the card on the mantelpiece giving her next appointment at out-patients, but she found herself unable to speak. She tried, but no words came. Then she heard Janice going on in her silly way about the nighties, 'all brand new and never worn', and that was when she smiled. Of course they were new, specially chosen for this occasion. Already she had moved away from Janice, and soon she would be out of the reach of all social workers trying to make her do things she didn't want to do, like going down to 'the Centre', buying fresh vegetables and taking a holiday.

The only disappointment was that there was no bell ringing on the ambulance, as she had sometimes heard that exciting clamour at lunchtime, when there had been an accident somewhere near the office. It was all very quiet and efficient, the way the ambulance men lifted her up and laid her down and called her 'dear', and said she wasn't much of a weight. But when she found herself at the hospital there seemed to be a crowd of young doctors round her bed, so they must have thought she was important. Marcia didn't recognize any of them from the time before – housemen, she supposed, doing their six months on the wards, and perhaps one of them was the Registrar. Two of them examined her, but another couple, who presumably ought to have been attending, seemed to be talking about some dance they were going to or had been to, and that seemed wrong. She was certain that Mr Strong wouldn't approve of that.

Later, it must have been much later for she was now in a different place altogether and the young doctors had gone, she found herself wondering when she was going to see Mr Strong, and then worrying in case she might not be seeing him at all but some other surgeon or just an ordinary doctor. She must have spoken his name aloud, for the young round-faced nurse who was settling her pillows said, 'Don't you worry, Miss Ivory, Mr Strong'll be round in the morning.'

'Flowers for you, Miss Ivory! Well, somebody loves you, don't they?' It was a loud, bright voice that reminded Marcia rather of Janice, but of course it couldn't be Janice. 'Lovely, aren't they – chrysanths, and such an unusual shade. Shall I read the card for you, dear? You'll want to know who they're from. It says, "Letty, Norman and Edwin, with all good wishes and hopes for a speedy recovery". Isn't that nice!' In the nurse's mind Letty and Norman were a married couple with a little boy called Edwin, rather an unusual name, that, as uncommon as the pinky-mauve chrysanthemums.

Marcia smiled but did not comment, and the nurse did not expect her to. Poor soul, she was hardly up to that. Some hopes for a 'speedy recovery'!

The woman in the next bed looked at Marcia with interest. It livened things up a bit when a new patient came in, but Marcia just lay with her eyes closed so it wouldn't be much use trying to have a chat with her. Funny that she should have had those flowers when she looked the kind of person who wouldn't get any, and now two more lots had arrived. The nurse read out the cards again – one from 'Janice' (a posy of anemones), and the other (mixed garden flowers) from 'Priscilla and Nigel – so sorry to hear you're ill – get well soon'. Well, it didn't look as if *that* was likely to happen, judging by her appearance. And when they weighed her she was only six stone.

There was a stir at the end of the ward – Mr Strong was approaching with an entourage of young doctors, and Sister wheeling a filing cabinet of case notes. 'He's coming, dear,' Marcia's neighbour whispered, but Marcia still lay with closed eyes, apparently unconscious. All the same, she knew that he was taller than the young doctors accompanying him and that he was wearing a green tie.

'Well, Miss Ivory, we didn't expect to see you again so soon.' Mr Strong's tone was kindly rather than reproachful, but she couldn't help wondering if she had displeased him in some way, for when she opened her eyes she saw that he was looking down at her, frowning a little. Then he turned to Sister and said something in a low voice.

'You've lost a lot of weight. Haven't you been looking after yourself properly?' This time there was a hint of sternness in his voice.

Marcia wanted to tell him that she had never been a big eater but she found it impossible to get out the words.

'Never mind – don't try to talk.' Mr Strong then turned to one of the young doctors. 'Well, Brian, you've got her notes – let's have your diagnosis.'

Brian, a youth with blond bobbed hair, said something in medical jargon but apparently Mr Strong was not satisfied because he turned to one of the other doctors for his opinion. This young man was even more at a loss than Brian. He mumbled something to the effect that the patient was in 'a terminal situation', a euphemism which fortunately meant nothing to Marcia who was conscious only of a flood of words. They were having quite a discussion about her.

'You're talking about me,' she said, almost in a whisper.

'Yes – you're certainly the centre of attraction today.' But Mr Strong said it so nicely, not in a nasty, sarcastic way, as Norman might have done.

'If they said "No visitors" then we can't very well barge in,' Norman pointed out, as he and Edwin sat in the office finishing their lunch. Jelly babies being in short supply, Edwin offered a packet of liquorice allsorts and Norman selected a brown and black one.

'I always think of her at coffee time,' Norman went on, 'the way she used to make coffee for me.'

'She used to make it for herself as well, not just for you,' Edwin corrected him.

'That's right – spoil my romantic memories,' said Norman flippantly. 'Poor old girl – not even allowed visitors. What did the nurse say when you rang?'

'She said Miss Ivory was quite comfortable, what they always say.' His wife Phyllis, on the point of death, had been 'comfortable' and perhaps that was one way of putting it. 'They want her to be kept very quiet, no excitement.'

'Yes, I suppose seeing us might be that – excitement,' Norman remarked.

'Oh, and Sister said how pleased she was with the flowers – such an unusual shade.'

'Did Marcia say that?'

'No, I don't think she did – that's what Sister thought. I gathered Marcia wasn't talking much herself. She certainly wasn't when we found her like that.'

'She wasn't much of a talker when she was here,' Norman mused. 'I wonder what they'll do with her now.'

'Sister didn't say whether she was to have an operation or anything like that,' said Edwin. 'I suppose we'll just have to wait and see. I'll keep in touch. By the way, it was a bit awkward. When I called round with the flowers they asked me if I knew whether she had any relatives, who would be her next of kin.'

'She must have given some name when she had her operation. I think she's got a distant cousin somewhere, she once said.'

'Oh, has she?' Edwin seemed a little embarrassed. 'I think they wanted somebody on the spot, as it were, so I had to give myself,' he admitted. 'I said I was her next of kin.' Saying the words like that seemed to open up endless possibilities.

'Sooner you than me!' said Norman roughly. 'Goodness knows what you may have let yourself in for.'

'Oh, I think it will just be a question of keeping in touch and that sort of thing. I felt it was the least I could do.'

'Let's hope it won't turn out to be the most,' said Norman in a dark tone.

'No visitors? Has she just had an operation, then?' Mrs Pope wanted to know.

'I don't think so. Just what Sister said, I gather,' said Letty.

'Well, we know what *that* means. You mark my words.'

Letty had realized by now that Mrs Pope's words invariably did have to be marked. 'I should like to go and see her,' she said, but uncertainly, for she did not really want to visit Marcia in hospital, only felt that she ought to want to.

'You won't be able to do that,' said Mrs Pope.

'I suppose not, as things are at present. I must think of something to send her, apart from flowers.' But what? she wondered, remembering Marcia as she had last seen her. Toilet water, talcum powder, some really nice soap – these were the things Letty herself would have liked if she had been in hospital, but would Marcia? 'Perhaps a book,' she said doubtfully.

'A book?' Mrs Pope's tone rang out scornfully. 'What would she want with a book if she's not allowed visitors?'

'No, perhaps she wouldn't be able to read,' Letty admitted. And had Marcia ever read anyway, ever been seen with a book? Her visits to the library had been for quite other purposes. She was the kind of person who would say that she didn't have time to read – yet hadn't she once, surprisingly, quoted a tag of poetry, some left-over fragment of her school days that had stuck in her memory? Perhaps a book of poetry, then, a paperback with a pretty cover, nothing modern, of course . . . Letty toyed with this idea but in the end she decided on a bottle of lavender water, the kind of thing that could be dabbed on the brow of a patient not allowed visitors.

'If she's as bad as I think she is,' Mrs Pope went on, 'she won't notice whether you send her anything or not. And you are a pensioner – don't forget that.'

'All the same, I do feel I'd like to send her something,' Letty said, irritated by Mrs Pope's attitude. 'After all, we did work together all those years.' Two women working together in an office, she thought, even if they didn't become close friends, would have a special kind of tie linking them – all the dull routine, the petty grumbles and the shared irritation of the men.

'I thought it was only two or three years,' said Mrs Pope. 'Not a long time.'

'Yes, but it was an important stage in our lives,' said Letty, deciding definitely on lavender water.

Lavender. Mr Strong detected the scent of it above the hospital smells. It reminded him of his grandmother, not at all the kind of thing one associated with Miss Ivory, but on the other hand why should he have been surprised that Miss Ivory should smell of lavender? The really surprising thing was that he should have noticed anything at all like that about a patient, but the scent, that powerful evocator of memory, had caught him unaware, and for a brief moment he – consultant surgeon at this eminent London teaching hospital and with a lucrative private practice in Harley Street – was a boy of seven again.

Somebody had been fussing over her, tidying her up because Mr Strong was coming round, and we wanted to look tidy for Mr Strong, didn't we? There was a cool, wet feeling on her forehead. Somebody – Betty or Letty, was it, on the card? – had sent her this nice lavender water, such a lovely fresh smell, like a country garden. Miss Ivory had a garden, hadn't she, and did she have lavender in her garden? Marcia hadn't been able to remember whether she had or not; she only remembered the catmint at the bottom of the garden and how she hadn't been able to find Snowy's grave. All that time she had watched him growing cold until the fleas left his body, and now she couldn't find his grave. It would have been much more to the point if Nigel from next door had helped her to find that rather than fuss about cutting her grass which didn't really need cutting because she preferred it that way; it kept people out. One afternoon, she couldn't exactly remember when, she had caught Norman spying on her, hanging about in the road. She regretted now that she hadn't gone up to him and challenged him, asked him what he thought he was doing, loitering with intent, outside her house. Another time, when she had first gone to work in the office, she had followed him one lunchtime all the way to the British Museum, up the steps and along to that place where they had the mummies, and seen him sitting looking at the mummified animals with a crowd of school children. She had gone away, not knowing what to think ... After that she had taken to making him coffee because it seemed silly for them each to get a tin when the big economy size was so much cheaper ... But after that? She was confused – nothing seemed to have happened after that. She moved her head restlessly from side to side. She thought she could see the chaplain coming towards her, the hospital chaplain, or was it the trendy vicar from the church at the end of the road? They were both young, with that long hair. No, it was neither; it was Mr Strong's houseman; his name was Brian. It was nice the way Mr Strong called all the young doctors by their Christian names – Brian and Geoffrey and Tom and Martin, and Jennifer, the only girl among them.

The young doctor bent over Marcia. He didn't like the look of her at all – indeed she was the kind of patient one didn't like the look of at the best of times. Luckily Mr Strong was still around and it took only a minute to get him back again. He had been very concerned about Miss Ivory and would want to be around if anything happened.

Mr Strong was still wearing that green tie – was it the same tie or did he just like the colour green? It had a small, close design on it. His rather bushy eyebrows were drawn together over his grey eyes in a frown. He always seemed to be frowning – had she done something wrong? Not eaten enough, perhaps? His eyes seemed to bore into her – the piercing eyes of the surgeon, did people say that? No, it was rather the surgeon's hands that people noticed and commented on, like the hands of a pianist when, at a concert, people tried to sit where they could see the pianist's hands. But in a sense the surgeon was just as much of an artist, that beautiful neat scar . . . Marcia remembered what her mother used to say, how she would never let the surgeon's knife touch her body. How ridiculous that seemed when one considered Mr Strong! . . . Marcia smiled and the frown left his face and he seemed to be smiling back at her.

The chaplain, on his way to visit Miss Ivory, was told that he was too late. 'Miss Ivory's gone, passed on . . .' The words rang in his head like a television advertisement jingle, but he prayed for the repose of her soul and nerved himself for the meeting with her next of kin and other relatives. But the man he eventually saw didn't seem to be any relation at all, just a 'friend' who was stepping into the breach, as it were. Somebody who had worked in the same office. Rather surprisingly, he held the view that there was nothing to reproach oneself with for not having been able to prevent death when, for the Christian, it was so much to be desired. Everything concerning Miss Ivory was settled with calm efficiency, without recriminations and certainly without tears, and that was a great relief.

Twenty

'CHAPELS OF REPOSE or Rest, is that what they call them?' said Norman. 'The place where the deceased is put,' he added awkwardly, not quite accustomed to thinking of Marcia dead.

'It's rather nice,' Letty murmured, 'to put it like that, the idea of resting.' When her mother had died the body had remained in the house before the funeral. Letty could only remember feeling drained of emotion and worried about practical details, distant relatives suddenly appearing, and the arrangements for their lunch.

'Well, here we are all together today, just like we used to be,' said Edwin, but the others made no comment, for it was not quite like they used to be.

The three of them were having a cup of coffee in Edwin's house before the funeral service at the crematorium, for which he had made all the arrangements. Marcia's death had of course brought them closer together, for they were remembering their past association and perhaps wondering whether one of them would be the next to go, but not too seriously because they were all in good health and they had known about Marcia's operation and what it could lead to. The most important thing was that they were seeing Edwin's house for the first time, never having been invited into it before. Death has done this, Letty thought, looking around her with a woman's critical eye at the old-fashioned embroidered cushion covers and chair backs – Phyllis's work on those long evenings when Edwin was at meetings of the parochial church council? Norman's reflections were more of a practical and financial nature – that Edwin could take a lodger or even two and get quite a nice bit coming in per week for a business gentleman, perhaps sharing the kitchen. Not that he would fancy sharing with Edwin if it came to that, which it obviously wouldn't. The fact that Edwin lived in this house alone meant that he had no need of extra cash, that he wouldn't be dependent on his pension when the time came.

It was a long car ride to the crematorium in the south-east corner of London, and as time went on conversation between the three of them began to flow more easily.

'After all,' Edwin pointed out, 'we're taking Marcia with us, we must think of it like that, and she wouldn't be saying much anyway, so we can talk between ourselves in the ordinary way.'

This invitation to ordinary talk seemed to stun them into silence, then Letty made a remark about the roses, still beautiful in a garden they happened to be passing.

'Little did we think, that time we all had lunch together,' said Edwin.

'Poor old girl – she seemed a bit round the bend then, didn't she?' said Norman.

'I suppose that must have been the beginning of the end,' said Letty. 'She hardly ate anything, just a bit of salad.'

'Oh, well, she was never a big eater,' said Norman, as if he was the only one to be let into this secret. 'She often used to say.'

'Living alone sometimes makes people not bother about meals,' said Edwin, almost as if solitude was a state that none of them had experience of.

'I always see to it that I get one good meal a day,' said Letty.

'Mrs Pope lets you use her kitchen, of course,' said Edwin. 'Do you use your own cooking utensils?'

'I have a couple of non-stick saucepans and my own omelette pan,' said Letty, hurrying over the words, for she felt that the conversation was getting rather too ordinary now and she did not want to hear about Norman's frying pan.

'Oh, I just shove everything into the frying pan,' Norman said, as she knew he would. 'Omelettes and all. Not that you can really call it an omelette, the kind of egg thing I make.'

The hearse was gathering speed now, so the car following could step on it a bit, Norman thought. It was quite clever the way they did it, gradually increasing the speed. It would be a skilled form of driving, that, and no doubt the cars were automatic. Ken would know and it might be something to talk to him about next time they met; conversation was not his strong point except where it concerned the motor car.

'Are we nearly there?' Letty asked. 'I don't know this part of London.'

'I brought Phyllis here,' said Edwin, in a matter-of-fact way. 'It's the nearest crematorium for where I live.'

'Oh, yes, of course.' Letty was momentarily embarrassed but Edwin did not seem to be affected by the memory of his dead wife, only going on to say that they had had a service at the church first which had been very well attended.

Edwin consulted his watch. 'Eleven thirty is our time,' he said, 'and I think they work to a pretty tight schedule. Oh, there's Father G.'s car just in front – he must have nipped past us at the traffic lights.'

'Crossed on the amber, I shouldn't wonder,' said Norman.

'This must be it,' said Letty, relieved that the end of the drive seemed to be in sight. 'Those gates ahead of us?'

'Yes, that's it,' Edwin confirmed.

'What we all come to,' Norman said.

*

'*Poor* Miss Ivory,' Priscilla whispered to Janice. 'I'm glad I was able to come, neighbours, and all that – and to give you moral support.'

Janice was not sure that she liked the way Priscilla had put it, as if she *needed* moral support, but probably she had just meant for the service at the crematorium which wasn't an everyday thing. For there was no question of Janice needing moral support in any other way. The discovery of Miss Ivory's slumped body in the kitchen and her subsequent death in hospital, although unusual, not to say unfortunate, in no way reflected on the social services and there could be no implication of neglect on Janice's part. Death was the end of all things, the culmination of life, and so it was for Marcia Ivory, a fitting conclusion to her story – something that could be quoted in years to come as an example of the kind of difficulties encountered by the voluntary social worker. It was impossible to help some people, to guide them in the way they should go for their own good, and Miss Ivory had certainly been one of those. Janice's thoughts clothed themselves in the language of a report, for it did appear from what one of the doctors at the hospital had said that Miss Ivory had quite definitely been in a terminal situation, even before her last collapse. The only trouble was that there might possibly have been a lack of liaison, that Miss Ivory might be said to have fallen through the net, that dreaded phrase . . .

Letty, noticing Janice and Priscilla in their rather too bright everyday clothes, realized that she need not have worried about not having anything suitable for a funeral – obviously younger people didn't take any notice of that kind of thing nowadays. Her dark-blue dress and jacket was sober, but hardly mourning; the saleswoman where she bought it had called the colour 'French navy', which seemed to add an old-fashioned touch of frivolity. The men were of course wearing black ties, for presumably a black tie was the kind of thing a man always had or could easily obtain.

Requiescat in pace, and may light perpetual shine upon her, Edwin thought. It had been a good idea to get Father G. to officiate at the brief service. He could ensure that things were done decently and in order, which one rather suspected some of these clergy officiating at crematoria, having to do one funeral after another, didn't always achieve. He was glad to see that that social worker and the neighbour had put in an appearance, it was the least they could do, but undoubtedly it was just as well it had been him and Father G., rather than them or poor old Norman, who had discovered Marcia lying like that.

Norman, strangely disturbed by the idea of Marcia lying in her coffin about to be consigned to the flames, was visited by a frivolous couplet he had read somewhere:

Dust to dust, ashes to ashes.
Into the grave the great Queen dashes.

He didn't know whether to laugh, which you could hardly do here, or cry, which you couldn't do either and it was a long time since he had shed tears. He bent his head, as the curtains closed and the coffin slid away, not wanting to see that last bit.

Afterwards they all gathered outside in an awkward little group in the bright sunshine.

'What lovely flowers,' Letty murmured, turning to Janice and Priscilla. The eternal usefulness of flowers again eased a strained situation. Two sheaves of flame gladioli and pink and white carnations and two wreaths of hot-house roses, mauve everlastings and white chrysanthemums were lying in a space bearing a notice which proclaimed 'Marcia Joan Ivory'.

'Priscilla and I thought she'd rather have cut flowers,' said Janice a little defiantly, her eyes on the wreaths. 'Some people do specify that.'

'Poor old Marcia, she was hardly in a state to specify anything,' Norman said. 'We clubbed together for a wreath – the mauve and white – Letty, Edwin and I, seeing as how . . .'

'Of course, you worked together, didn't you?' said Priscilla, in her best finishing-school manner. She didn't quite know how to cope with this odd little man and the other hardly less odd tall one, and hoped that it would be possible to get away quickly now that she had done her social duty.

'The other wreath is from Marcia's cousin,' said Edwin. 'She did have this distant cousin but she was too upset to attend the funeral.'

'Not having seen her for forty years,' Norman chipped in.

'The son came, though,' said Edwin, 'so that was something. Apparently he works in London.'

'That young person sitting at the back?' said Letty. She had noticed somebody of indeterminate sex, with straggling, tow-coloured hair, wearing a kaftan.

'Yes, wearing a bead necklace, that's him.'

The group dispersed. Edwin, Letty and Norman found their way to Father G., who was waiting rather impatiently by his car. Edwin sat in the front by Father G. and Letty and Norman squashed into the back with the suitcase containing his vestments. The two in front kept up an animated conversation, mostly church shop, but the two in the back were silent. Norman did not know what to say or even what he felt, except that funerals were sad occasions anyway, but Letty was overcome by a sense of desolation, as if by Marcia's death she was now completely alone. And it wasn't even as if they had been close friends.

Twenty-one

'Little did we think...'

It was inevitable that Norman should say something of the kind, Letty felt, remembering the last time they had eaten a meal together in a restaurant. Little, indeed, had they thought on that occasion at the Rendezvous that the next time would be like this. Now of course they had Father G. with them, so that added something different.

'Well, now...' Father G. took up the menu and began to study it. He presumed that he and Edwin would be sharing the cost of the meal between them, Letty being a woman, and Norman something a little less than the kind of man one might expect to treat one to a lunch. He had wondered when the funeral arrangements were being made what the aftermath was going to be, seeing that the deceased appeared to have no relative capable of laying on funeral baked meats. At first he had wondered if Edwin himself would invite them all back to his house, but he was relieved that he had evidently decided against it but had chosen a nearby restaurant with a licence. It was an agreeable change not to be crowded into a suburban sitting room or 'lounge', invariably furnished in appalling taste, forced to drink sweet sherry or the inevitable cups of tea. Would it be in the least appropriate, he wondered, to suggest what he really felt like at this moment – a dry Martini?

'Something to drink, I feel,' said Edwin, echoing Father G.'s thought.

'Yes, one does feel . . .' Letty murmured.

'It takes it out of you, a day like this,' Norman said awkwardly. He had been going to say that what takes it out of you is a funeral but somehow the word did not come, as if he did not like to think of it, let alone say the word out loud.

Father G., thus encouraged, felt justified in being brisk and taking action. He summoned a waiter and ordered drinks – medium sherry for Edwin and Norman, a dry Martini for himself, and for the lady . . . Letty's hesitation, her slight feeling that perhaps they ought not to be drinking when poor Marcia had never touched a drop, was taken by Father G. to be womanly modesty or ignorance of what was available. 'Why not try a dry Martini?' he suggested. 'That will pull you together.'

'Yes, I do feel as if I needed something like that,' she agreed, and when the drink came it did seem to achieve a kind of pulling together. There is something in it, she thought, the comfort of drink at a time like this. It also had the effect of making her realize that while poor Marcia was no longer with them she and the others were very much alive – Edwin, his usual grey solemn self, Norman, obviously in a state of some emotion, and Father G., the efficient bossy clergyman. Looking round the restaurant, she noticed an arrangement of artificial sweet peas in unnaturally bright colours, a party of businessmen at a long table, and two smartly dressed women comparing patterns of curtain material. Conscious of her own aliveness, she allowed Father G. to persuade her to choose oeufs Florentine, because it sounded attractive, while he himself had a steak, Edwin grilled plaice, and Norman cauliflower au gratin. 'I don't feel like much,' Norman added, subtly making the others feel that they ought not to have felt like much either.

'You've retired now?' Father G. asked, making conversation with Letty. 'That must be . . .' he cast about for a word to describe what Letty's retirement must be . . . 'a great opportunity,' he brought out, all life being nothing so much as a great opportunity.

'Yes, it certainly is!' The dry Martini had encouraged Letty to a greater appreciation of her present state. 'I find I can do all sorts of things now.'

'We could take that in more ways than one,' said Norman, with a return of his usual jaunty manner. 'It makes us wonder what you get up to.'

'Nothing, really,' said Letty, inhibited by the presence of Father G. 'I just have more time to do things – reading and other kind of work.'

'Ah, yes, social work.' Father G. nodded approvingly.

'I think Letty is more likely to be on the receiving end of the social worker's ministrations,' said Edwin. 'After all, she *is* a retired person, a senior citizen, you might say.'

Letty felt it a little unfair of Edwin to lump her into this category, when she had hardly any grey hairs in spite of her age, and Father G. seemed to draw away from her at this unattractive classification. He did not much care for the aged, the elderly, or just 'old people', whatever you liked to call them.

'What about the next course?' Edwin asked.

'Do you remember the last time?' Norman asked suddenly. 'What we had then?'

'I think you and I had apple pie and ice cream,' Letty said.

'That's right – Aunt somebody's apple pie. Edwin had the cream caramel and he tried to get Marcia to have some but she wouldn't.'

There was silence and for a moment nobody could think of anything else to say. They may all have been aware that at a time of bereavement it is best not to bottle things up. Marcia's name had not been mentioned up to now and perhaps it was fitting that Norman should be the one to bring it out.

'She always had such a small appetite,' Letty said at last.

'Never a big eater.' Norman's voice seemed as if it might break on these words but he controlled himself.

I must ask him round to a meal one evening, Edwin thought, give him a chance to talk about her if he wants to. He did not much look forward to the prospect but things like this had to be done and one couldn't expect always to enjoy doing one's Christian duty.

'What is going to happen to Miss Ivory's house?' asked Father G., as if the mention of property might bring the conversation up to a higher level. 'I suppose it will be left to that – er – relative?'

'The young man in the bead necklace or his mother, I suppose,' said Edwin. 'I believe those were her only relatives.'

'If it were smartened up a bit it would be quite a desirable property,' Father G. said, in a condescending estate-agent's tone.

'What do you mean, if it was smartened a bit?' Norman asked aggressively.

Father G. smiled. 'Well, you know, it could have done with a lick of paint – that was my impression. Now, what about some ice cream?' he asked in a soothing tone, feeling that ice cream might act like oil on troubled waters and pacify the angry Norman more effectively than any words of his.

'We finished off with ice cream,' Letty said. 'There were so many different kinds, it was like being a child again. Even Norman said he'd always liked strawberry ice. I think it cheered him up in a sort of way.'

'I couldn't decide whether you'd be hungry or not,' Mrs Pope said. 'One never knows after a funeral.'

Letty was surprised and obscurely comforted to realize that

Mrs Pope had been thinking of her to the extent of wondering whether she would need a meal. The time – just after five o'clock – was an unpromising one for anything except a 'high tea' and that seemed inappropriate.

'Edwin seemed to know this restaurant quite near, so that was very convenient,' Letty explained.

Mrs Pope had been waiting expectantly, so Letty had to tell her what they had eaten. Steak for Father G. had seemed suitable, for after all he had taken the service and in some way, Mrs Pope commented, the clergy appeared to relish meat and even to need it. Oeufs Florentine, Letty's choice, sounded frivolous and unfeeling, on a par with wearing something in 'French navy' to the funeral. What was it about the French, or the idea of the French? Surely now that we were a part of the EEC things would be different, attitudes would change? Or would we be infected by their supposed frivolity? So Letty just said that she had had 'an egg dish'.

'Well, eggs are as nourishing as meat in their way,' Mrs Pope pronounced, 'so you probably won't feel like another egg now.'

'I think just a cup of tea...' There was something to be said for tea and a comfortable chat about crematoria.

Twenty-two

NORMAN WENT INTO Marcia's house, using the front door key which had been handed over to him by the solicitor. He entered 'the dwelling of Miss Marcia Joan Ivory, deceased'. That was how he put it to himself and how, shocked into his usual flippancy, he had discussed with Edwin the astonishing news that Marcia had left her house to him. The will had evidently been made just after her operation, at a time when she had been forced to face up to the future. Her money, such as it was, had been left to her cousin, with a legacy for the son. 'He'll be able to buy himself another string of beads,' was Norman's comment.

'Norman, the Man of Property,' Edwin teased, and it seemed to redress the balance between them, now that Norman also had a house and need no longer be an object of pity, alone in his bed-sitter. Yet it would really have been more suitable if Marcia had left her house to Letty, also alone in a bedsitter though she did have the company of Mrs Pope. 'Are you going to live in it?' Edwin asked, remembering the state the house had been in when he and Father G. had gone in that time. 'It'll need a bit doing to it,' he couldn't resist adding. 'I shouldn't be surprised if the roof leaked.'

'Oh, so what!' said Norman. 'Who cares about the roof?'

‘Well, water might come in – rain and snow.’

‘We don’t get much snow in London, not south of the river, anyway.’

‘Did you know about this – had you any idea?’

‘What do you think? Of course I hadn’t.’

‘She used to make coffee for you, remember,’ Edwin persisted.

‘That was only because she thought it cheaper to share the large economy tin, as you’ve already pointed out more than once,’ Norman retorted angrily.

They had parted slightly annoyed with each other, and the next day Norman had taken a day off to go and look at the house. He had a few extra bits of leave still owing to him, so there was no difficulty about that. Who would ever have thought that one of those extra days would have come in useful on this sort of occasion? God moves in a mysterious way, his wonders to perform, and you could certainly call this a wonder.

The key fitted easily in the Yale lock and there was a mortise lock too. Marcia had been careful about burglars, especially when she was out all day. Standing in the hall, Norman noticed the solid Edwardian furniture – hatstand, table and chairs – rather than the dust over everything, for of course it would be dusty after all this time, stands to reason, he said to himself. He wandered from room to room, seeing not himself in possession but Marcia as she must have been in the time he had known her but never been invited here. If she had invited him, would things have been any different? But she never would have invited him – that was the essence of their relationship. So it had been a relationship, had it? He remembered that time she had followed him into the BM, and he had been trapped in front of those animals, gaping at them with a crowd of school kids, stuck there until it was safe to go. She thought he hadn’t seen her, but he had, and after that he hadn’t gone to the museum again, just trotted off to the library. Then there had been the making of the coffee, that Edwin was always going on about – there hadn't really been much in that...

Norman ascended the stairs. He came into a room that might have been her bedroom. It had shabby, rose-flowered wallpaper and a faded patterned carpet. There was a table by the bed, and on it some books, an anthology of poetry, which surprised him, and a collection of pamphlets, the sort of thing you got in the library, giving details of services available for the retired and elderly. There was an old, rather dirty white candlewick cover over the bed and the sheets and pillows were still on it, just as they had been. This was the bed where she had slept, where she had dreamed, and where she had reached the point of death, though she hadn't actually died in it. Edwin and Father G. had found her downstairs, sitting at the kitchen table.

Norman advanced to the dressing table, with its swinging mirror, which stood in the window. So she had wanted a good light to see her face in, a cruelly revealing light, showing every line? Yet Marcia hadn't been one to look much at herself in the glass, he suspected. She hadn't seemed to care much about her appearance at the best of times, even with the dyed hair. At the end, Sister had said something about her lovely *white* hair, so perhaps the dye had grown out by then and somebody had cut off the dark ends. She had looked quite beautiful, Sister said, so calm and peaceful, but no doubt they always said that to the relatives, they must have to do quite a lot of what he thought of as soft-soaping in hospitals – Marcia looking beautiful – that would be the day! Yet, now that he knew that she had left him the house, he was prepared to believe that she might have been almost beautiful.

There was a chest of drawers, presumably containing her clothes and her bits and pieces. He didn't particularly want to see those but he was drawn by curiosity. Tentatively, as if he were violating the sanctity of her secret office drawer, he opened one of the drawers. To his surprise, it was full of plastic bags of various sizes, all neatly folded and classified by size and type. There was something almost admirable about the arrangement, unexpected and yet just the sort of thing he could imagine Marcia doing.

He closed the drawer and stood in the middle of the room, wondering what to do. Surely he couldn't be expected to cope with all her mess, it was a woman's job. Letty ought to be here, sorting out the things, deciding what to do with the clothes. Perhaps he should get in touch with her, that was the obvious thing, unless the distant cousin could be approached; perhaps as a relative she had a prior claim. She had been too upset to attend the funeral but a few perks, like clothes and the odd stick of furniture, might work wonders on her sensibility.

Thinking about this, Norman moved into another room and stood looking out of a side window. From here he had a view of well-maintained and painted houses and neat gardens, the residences of his future neighbours, should he decide to live in the house himself.

'There's a man looking out of the window,' said Priscilla. 'He's in Miss Ivory's house. Do you suppose it's all right?'

'Perhaps we ought to investigate,' said Janice. She and Priscilla were sitting on the patio, drinking coffee. It was a marvellously sunny October day, a real Indian summer. Janice had been going to visit one of her cases in a nearby street, but the old person had been taken off for a drive by one of the enthusiastic amateur do-gooders from the church – annoying, the way social-services wires sometimes got crossed, though it meant that she had an unexpectedly free morning. So she had dropped in on Priscilla for a welcome cup of coffee and a gossip. Not exactly gossip, more to speculate on what might happen to Miss Ivory's house, what sort of neighbours Nigel and Priscilla might be getting.

'It looks like one of those men who were at the funeral,'

Priscilla said. 'You know, the men who worked in that office place.'

'What would he be doing in the house?' Janice asked. 'He never came to see Miss Ivory when she was alive.' Her tone reflected some of the indignation she felt at the idea that Miss Ivory might have had friends who were perfectly capable of visiting her but never did. Yet wasn't it her job, her justification, her *raison d'être,* the loneliness of people like Miss Ivory? You couldn't have it all ways, as her husband sometimes reminded her. If the friends and relatives did their stuff, Janice might well be out of a job.

'Why don't we go over and see,' said Priscilla boldly. 'We can always say we noticed somebody in the house and wondered if it was all right. After all, we don't know him from Adam, do we?'

That social worker and her friend, the woman who lives next door, Norman thought, as he saw them coming to the house. What do *they* want?

'Yes?' he barked in a brusque, unpromising way, as he opened the front door an unfriendly crack.

Such an odd little man, thought Priscilla, preparing to assume her coolest social manner, but Janice got in first.

'I'm Janice Brabner,' she said, 'and I used to look after Miss Ivory.' Rather a pointless thing to say, she realized, as it might appear that she hadn't been all that successful. 'We saw somebody at an upstairs window,' she went on quickly.

'Yes, me,' said Norman. 'It's my house now. Miss Ivory left it to me in her will.'

Norman was prepared for the gasp of unflattering astonishment that met his announcement. It seemed as if they hardly believed him. The one called 'Priscilla' was a tall blonde, wearing velvet trousers, and the other (I'm Janice Brabner, he mimicked to himself) was shorter and squatter, a real bossy social-worker type. She was the first one to speak, after he had dropped his bombshell.

'Are you sure?' she said.

'Sure? Of course I'm sure!' Norman retorted indignantly.

'Oh, that is nice,' said Priscilla. She was not so stupid as to imagine that gushing social insincerity would get her anywhere with Norman, but it had occurred to her that if this person was going to be their new neighbour it would be just as well to get on to good terms with him. All the same she very much hoped that he wasn't going to be. What she really wanted was a young couple of about the same age as herself and Nigel, perhaps with children, so that they could do mutual baby-sitting when she and Nigel decided to start a family. The sort of people one could ask to dinner, which this odd little man, and whatever friends he might have, hardly seemed to be.

But Janice, with no stake in the future, could afford to be blunter. 'Are you going to live here?' she asked, straight out.

'I haven't made up my mind,' Norman said. 'I might decide to live here, and again I might not.'

At this stage the two women moved away, leaving Norman feeling that he had got the better of them. He did not go into the house again but began to explore that garden – 'explore' was the word, he decided, when you almost had to hack your way through the undergrowth. There was a garden shed, the kind of thing that might come in useful, and he saw himself arranging his tools and his 'gear' there. Perhaps Marcia had a lawn mower, a fork, a spade and a hoe, though it didn't look as if she had made much use of them lately. He pushed open the door of the shed. There were certainly some tools in one corner, but most of the space was taken up with rows of milk bottles stacked on shelves; there must have been over a hundred of them.

At this point Norman felt he couldn't cope any more. The small-scale stuffiness of his bedsitter seemed suddenly very cosy and attractively safe, so he decided to go back to it, 'home' as it still was. All the same, he was now a house owner and it was up to him to decide what to do with the property, whether to live in it himself or to sell it, and houses in that street were fetching a tidy sum judging by the others he had seen there. The fact that the decision rested with him, that he had the power to influence the lives of people like Priscilla and her husband, gave him a quite new, hitherto unexperienced sensation – a good feeling, like a dog with two tails, as people sometimes put it – and he walked to the bus stop with his head held high.

That same evening, on the other side of the common, Edwin returned from the office, wondering what sort of a day Norman had spent in what he still thought of as 'Marcia's house'. In other circumstances he might have strolled over there but tonight, being the 18th of October and St Luke's day, he was hoping to find an evening Mass somewhere. The lunchtime churches had yielded nothing, a sad contrast to the days when Father Thames, and later Father Bode, had attracted a crowd of office workers. Edwin also thought regretfully of another church where he had often gone in the past, which would have provided a splendid service, but that church was no more. A scandal in the early fifties – Edwin remembered it well – had put an end to the splendid services, the congregation had fallen away and in the end the church had been closed as redundant. An office block now stood on the spot where the air had once been filled with incense. It was a sad story, but the upshot of it was that there would be no St Luke's day evening Mass *there*. Luke, the beloved physician. You would have thought that the church opposite the hospital where Marcia had died would be filled with devout consultants – surgeons and physicians – housemen and nurses, on this day, but not a bit of it. The St Luke's there was the kind of church that had only the bare mimimum of Sunday services and nothing on weekdays. Now that he came to think of it, Edwin had grave suspicions that Mr Strong, Marcia's surgeon, was not any kind of churchgoer. Something he had said, some disparaging remark he had made about the chaplain

. . . Still, that didn't solve the problem of the St Luke's day service and eventually the idea had to be given up.

Then it occurred to Edwin that he might give Letty a ring. At the funeral he had got the impression that she was a bit lonely, even living with Mrs Pope. After all, though it had been a good idea for her to go there as a lodger, was the company of a woman in her eighties quite enough for Letty? With this idea in his mind, he went to the telephone and dialled the number, but it was engaged. He decided to leave it for today and try again tomorrow or whenever he happened to remember it. After all, there was no hurry.

Twenty-three

LETTY HAD AN old-fashioned respect for the clergy which seemed outmoded in the seventies, when it was continually being brought home to her that in many ways they were just like other men, or even more so. The emphasis on humanity, in which we all share, had been the burden of a sermon she had recently heard at Mrs Pope's church, as if the preacher were preparing his congregation for some particularly outrageous piece of behaviour. In his case it had been no more than the removal of some of the pews at the back of the church to provide a space where the younger children could be accommodated during the service, but of course it had been greeted with indignant opposition by some.

'He is determined to ride roughshod over us,' Mrs Pope declared.

Letty, shocked by the violence of Mrs Pope's concept, had been about to say a word in the vicar's favour, when the telephone rang. Had it been a moment earlier (or later) it would have been Edwin, prompted by a friendly gesture towards Letty's supposed loneliness, but as it happened it was Marjorie, 'that friend of yours who's going to marry that clergyman', as Mrs Pope sometimes put it. But now, it appeared, Marjorie was not going to marry him. What Letty gathered from the incoherent outburst was that for some reason – it was a bad line, and she could not gather exactly what the reason was – the engagement had been broken off.

'Beth Doughty,' Marjorie wailed. 'And I had no idea ...'

For a moment Letty couldn't remember who Beth Doughty was, then it came back to her. The warden of Holmhurst, the home for retired gentlefolk, that was Beth Doughty – the efficient woman with the rigid hairstyle, who poured such generous gins, who knew the kind of food David Lydell liked and remembered his passion for Orvieto. There was something shocking in the idea of two women competing for the love of a clergyman with the lure of food and wine, but the whole pattern slotted into place. Humanity in which we all share ...

When the telephone was at last laid down, the main point that emerged was that Letty must go to Marjorie as soon as possible. Not, of course, this evening – there was no suitable train – but first thing tomorrow morning.

'Well ...' Letty turned to the expectant Mrs Pope. 'That was my friend. He has broken off the engagement,' she said. 'It seems there's another woman – the warden of an old people's home.'

It sounded very bad, put like that, and the involvement, however indirectly, of 'old people' seemed particularly distressing.

'*Really* ...' Mrs Pope could think of nothing to say that would adequately express her feelings. Compared with this, the removal of a few pews from the back of her own church was as nothing. 'You will want to go to her, of course,' she added, not without a touch of envy.

'Yes, first thing in the morning,' said Letty. She felt curiously elated, a feeling she tried to suppress but it would not go away. She began to plan what sort of clothes she would take for this unexpected visit to Marjorie. The weather had been very warm for October, but she must remember that it was always colder in the country.

*

'His gastric trouble, and then there was his mother being over ninety, and in a way . . .' Marjorie hesitated, 'the age difference. He was some years younger than I am, of course.'

Letty murmured sympathetically, for she had known all these things and now that Marjorie was explaining what had happened, how he had seemed reluctant to fix the date of the wedding – it had already been put off once because of his mother's health – it seemed remarkable to consider that he had ever agreed to get married at all. And how had Beth Doughty managed it, for surely that needed to be explained? The other factors would still apply, and it wasn't as if she was much younger than Marjorie.

Marjorie didn't seem to know the answer to this or she was too upset to discuss the matter further. Letty began to wonder whether Beth Doughty might not also be rejected in her turn, whether no woman would succeed in bringing David Lydell to the point of marriage, but she did not say anything of this.

'You can't know what a woman is up to,' Marjorie said. 'It's something that can never be expected or explained.'

Letty agreed that this was very true and found herself thinking of Marcia leaving her house to Norman, a perfect example of the unpredictability of women. And now, with Marcia dead, her action could never be explained.

'Where will David Lydell go?' Letty asked.

'Go? That's almost the worst part of it – he won't be going anywhere. He'll be staying here.'

'He's decided to stay *here*?'

'I don't know about decided – I don't think he's considered moving.'

'Well, I suppose he hasn't been in the village very long, but in the circumstances . . .' Letty was uncertain of her ground here and felt unable to go any further. And yet, when one came to think of it, why should David Lydell leave the district? He had done nothing worse than change his mind and, as people were always saying, it was better to discover this kind of mistake sooner rather than later. 'Where will he live?' she went on. 'Surely not at the old people's home – at Holmhurst?'

'I don't think so – I suppose they'll move into the vicarage.'

That uncomfortable vicarage, that needed so much doing to it, Letty remembered. Perhaps it was just what he deserved. 'But won't it distress him to think of you alone here?' she said.

'Oh, Letty . . .' Marjorie's smile was indulgent, as if making allowances for her friend's unworldliness. 'Anyway, I have a feeling that I may not be alone for long.'

'Really?' This coy admission made Letty wonder what Marjorie could possibly mean. Surely it was much too soon for another likely husband to have appeared in the village?

'Why, don't you see . . .' Marjorie began to explain and then of course Letty did see. Now that there was to be no marriage the plans for Letty's retirement could be carried out as before, just as if nothing had happened to change them. She would (naturally) be moving into the country to join Marjorie as soon as arrangements could be made.

And then what? Letty wondered. Supposing after a few months or years Marjorie met somebody else to marry, what would happen to Letty then? In the past she had always trailed behind Marjorie, when the two of them were together, but there was no reason why this should always be the pattern. She decided that she would think the matter over, not make up her mind immediately.

'I suppose you've sent back his ring,' she said, deliberately returning to the matter of the broken engagement.

'Oh, goodness no – David wanted me to keep it. I suppose he could hardly have asked for it back, under the circumstances.'

'No, he couldn't have asked, but you might have felt you didn't want to keep it,' said Letty.

'But it's such a pretty ring, a moonstone in an antique setting. You know I've always wanted an antique ring,' Marjorie babbled on, saying how much more interesting such a ring was than the conventional small diamond of her first marriage. 'And when one's older, one's hands seem to thicken and the fingers get fatter, so a larger ring looks better.' She spread out her left hand, still wearing the moonstone, appraisingly for Letty to see.

Twenty-four

'Wonders will never cease – that's all I have to say.' Norman took a corned-beef sandwich out of a plastic bag.

'We've certainly had abundant proof of that,' said Edwin, busy with a tea bag. 'I had Mrs Pope on the telephone last night and she told me the whole story. Letty's friend rang up to say that the whole thing was off – she wasn't going to get married after all. Of course she was very upset – that's why Letty went down there.'

'What could *she* do? Listen to her friend going on about her loss, I suppose. Old Letty never strikes me as being much use in a crisis.'

'Perhaps she can't do all that much – but the presence of a woman friend . . .' Edwin hesitated, not knowing how to classify the type of comfort Letty might be capable of providing.

'Oh, yes, I agree – women certainly have their uses.'

'Especially if they leave you houses in their wills,' Edwin said, in a jocular tone. 'You must be getting quite used to being a property owner.'

'I'm going to sell it,' Norman said. 'I wouldn't fancy living in it.'

'Yes, that's the best thing – it would be much too big for you,' Edwin pointed out, reasonably enough.

'Oh, I don't know so much about that,' said Norman huffily. 'It's only an ordinary semi, you know, just like yours, and you don't find yours too big. I don't necessarily want to end my days in a bedsitter.'

'No, of course not.' Edwin's tone was the soothing one he generally used to pacify the angry little man.

'I suppose I'm more likely to end my days in an old people's home,' said Norman, taking up the large economy size of instant coffee. 'It says "Family Size" here – funny, really, when it's mostly used by people in offices.' He spooned coffee powder into a mug. 'Of course you do save a bit – that's what Marcia and I thought.'

Edwin made no comment. In his silence he agitated his tea bag with a spoon; a stream of amber-coloured liquid was released into the boiling water. Then he added the usual slice of lemon, stirred it and prepared to drink. Norman's words, the way he had said 'Marcia and I', had made him wonder whether the two of them could ever have married. Yet it was impossible to imagine how such an event could have been brought about. If they had met many years ago, when they were both younger? Apart from the difficulty of picturing them being younger, they probably wouldn't have been attracted to each other at that time, and even now the idea of 'attraction' seemed ridiculous when you applied it to Norman and Marcia. And yet what was it that brought people together, even the most unlikely people? Edwin had only the haziest memories of his own courtship and marriage, in the days when he had been a server at the spikiest Anglo-Catholic church where Phyllis was a member of the congregation. In the thirties people did get married in a way that they seemed not to now, or at least not to the same extent, he qualified. Supposing Marcia had not died, could she and Norman have married and lived in her house? It was something he felt he could not ask Norman...

But now Norman was breaking into Edwin's unspoken

thoughts and asking his advice about a matter that seemed to be troubling him.

'All those clothes and things, what am I to do about them?'

'How do you mean?'

'Marcia's clothes and the things in the house. Of course the nephew – the one in the kaftan and beads – was taking some odds and ends, but he said his mum didn't want to be bothered, said I was to do what I liked. *I* – I ask you!' Norman kicked the wastepaper basket with an angry gesture.

'What about that neighbour and the social worker – the ones who were at the funeral?'

'The sexy blonde and the bossy do-gooding bitch?' Irritation seemed to add violent colour to Norman's way of expressing himself. 'Catch me asking *them!*'

'Well, there must be somebody at the local church . . . somebody who could make use of them.'

'You *would* suggest that. No doubt your friend Father G. would come to the rescue.'

'I'm sure he would,' said Edwin, on the defensive. 'Old clothes are always welcome for jumble sales.'

'Jumble sales! Thank you very much! So that's what you think Marcia's clothes would be.'

'Well, you must admit the last time we saw her she did look a bit odd,' Edwin began, but then he stopped himself. This pointless bickering was getting them nowhere. Perhaps Norman was remembering Marcia differently now – a gracious white-haired woman with a sweet expression, as Sister had described her at the end. 'Have you thought of asking Letty?' he asked. 'I'm sure she would help.'

'Yes, that's an idea.' Norman seemed grateful. 'It would be better than having a stranger.'

*

'What are we going to do with all these milk bottles?' Edwin asked.

'I don't know,' said Norman. 'What would you do – just leave them?'

'I suppose I'd get rid of them gradually – put out a few for the milkman every day.'

'We could start by putting some out now,' Letty suggested.

'Yes, they're always telling us to rinse and return,' said Norman.

'And these are spotlessly clean,' Edwin pointed out.

'I wonder if Marcia would be angry to think of us doing this,' said Letty. 'She must have had some plan in mind, keeping them all in the shed, so beautifully washed and arranged.'

The three of them had spent an interesting afternoon in Marcia's house, going through her things. Letty had been most surprised at the clothes, stowed away in wardrobes and drawers, dresses of the thirties and earlier, now coming back into fashion, some of them obviously belonging to Marcia's mother. Things Marcia herself must have worn when she was young before any of them had known her. And there had also been clothes she must have bought comparatively recently, most of which seemed inexplicably unworn. Had she been keeping them for some special occasion which had never arisen? It was impossible to know now.

They had started their work upstairs, but when they came down to the kitchen it had been even more surprising to open the store cupboard and come upon such an array of tinned foods.

'Whatever can she have bought all this stuff for?' Edwin exclaimed.

'Well, you buy tinned stuff, don't you?' Norman was immediately on the defensive. 'What's so surprising about it?'

'But she never seemed to eat anything,' Letty said.

'Never a big eater, she used to say,' Norman reminded them.

'I suppose she was prudent, like Mrs Thatcher,' said Edwin. 'What with prices going up the way they have been...'

'And will continue to go up, whatever government is in power,' Norman snapped.

'So beautifully arranged and classified,' said Letty, with wonder in her tone. 'Meat and fish and fruit, and here soups and macaroni cheese and ravioli...'

'Light supper dishes,' said Norman. 'I'm very partial to macaroni cheese – it was a godsend when I had that time with my teeth.'

'Yes, it would be,' said Letty, her tone now warm with sympathy.

'I think Norman had better have this stuff,' said Edwin. 'After all, if the cousin and her son have given you the go-ahead...'

'Well, I suppose the son might have some – a young man living in a hippy pad would probably be glad of a few tins. Luckily he doesn't seem to know quite how many there are. Why don't we all take a few for ourselves now,' said Norman.

Hesitantly, for it seemed very wrong to be helping themselves to Marcia's store cupboard like this, the three of them began making their selection. In some subtle way this reflected their different characters. Edwin chose spam and stewing steak, Letty prawns and peach halves, Norman sardines, soup, butter beans and the macaroni cheese.

Then, in the bottom corner of the cupboard, they came upon a bottle of sherry, unopened. It was a Cyprus cream sherry, reputedly made from grapes growing in vineyards which had once belonged to the Queen of Sheba.

'Shall we open it?' Norman asked. 'Don't you think she must have meant it for us, perhaps for this very occasion?'

'She could hardly have imagined us all here like this,' Letty said. 'I mean, without her.'

'Perhaps we should do as Norman suggests,' said Edwin. 'After all, it may well have been what Marcia would have wished, given the exceptional circumstances.' That was perhaps the best way of putting it, for it wasn't quite like every day. And surely, he felt, if anyone could claim to know what Marcia might have meant or wished, could attempt to probe such a mystery, it might be Norman?

'Queen of Sheba,' said Norman, who had found glasses and was pouring out generous measures of the golden liquid, 'I like that! Here's to us, then.'

'I suppose you'll be moving down to the country, Letty, now that your friend's not getting married after all,' Edwin said, the glow of the drink adding to the pleasure he felt at the improvement in Letty's prospects. It seemed to round things off in a most satisfactory way.

'I haven't decided,' she said. 'I'm not at all sure that I want to live in the country now.'

'That's right,' said Norman, 'don't you do anything you don't want to do, or let anybody tell you what you ought to do. Make up your own mind. It's your life, after all.'

'But I thought you loved the country,' said Edwin, dismay in his tone, for surely all middle-aged or elderly women loved, or ought to love, the country?

'I don't think I *love* it exactly,' said Letty, thinking of the dead birds and mangled rabbits and the cruel-tongued village people. 'It was just that it seemed a suitable arrangement when we made it. Now I feel that I have a choice.' She took a long draught of the sweet sherry and experienced a most agreeable sensation, almost a feeling of power. She felt as Norman had felt when he discovered that he could influence the lives of other people by deciding whether to live in Marcia's house or not. Letty now realized that both Marjorie and Mrs Pope would be waiting to know what *she* had decided to do.

'But surely you don't want to stay in London?' Edwin persisted.

'I don't know. I shall have to think about it,' Letty said. 'Oh, and that reminds me,' she added, 'Marjorie wondered if you two would like a day in the country. We could all go down there for lunch.'

She could not help smiling, for from a practical point of view there was something slightly ludicrous in the picture of them all – Marjorie and Letty and the two men – squashed up together in the Morris.

'Those two friends of yours, the men you worked with in that office, Edwin and Norman,' Marjorie had said, lingering over the names, 'wouldn't it be rather nice to invite them down for a day?'

Any new interest that might take Marjorie's mind off her disappointment was to be encouraged, Letty felt, though it was difficult to think of Edwin and Norman as objects of romantic speculation, and two less country-loving people could hardly be imagined. But at least it made one realize that life still held infinite possibilities for change.